Anonymous

Hand Book of Games and Pastimes

Anonymous

Hand Book of Games and Pastimes

ISBN/EAN: 9783337427986

Printed in Europe, USA, Canada, Australia, Japan

Cover: Foto ©Andreas Hilbeck / pixelio.de

More available books at **www.hansebooks.com**

HAND BOOK

OF

GAMES AND PASTIMES.

A MANUAL FOR PARLOR AND LAWN

COMPRISING A CHOICE COLLECTION

—OF—

Parlor Games, Tricks, Dialogues,

TABLEAUX,

RULES FOR LAWN TENNIS, CALLS FOR DANCING,

PALMISTRY, ETC., ETC.

CONTENTS.

INTRODUCTORY.

In preparing this book for the public our aim has been to place within the hands of every lady the means of making her home a pleasant one for all visitors, and also to give her some important hints concerning her health and beauty, which she may have been wholly ignorant of.

THE GAMES AND PASTIMES which we describe require no elaborate preparations. They are intended for Parlor and Lawn, as the title of the book will indicate, and are selected with a view to simplicity. We have inserted nothing which is difficult to learn.

Every one knows how hard it is sometimes, even on occasions of great festivity, like weddings, or birth-day parties, to make the company feel quite at home. Especially is this true where there are strangers among them. In such cases if the hostess will but set things moving by starting one of the games given in this book, it will take but a short time before everybody is on terms of easy familiarity with everybody else.

This alone would make the book valuable. But, as it is not our purpose to praise it, we will ask you to read it through, feeling sure you will appreciate its merits.

CHICAGO CORSET CO.

HAND BOOK

—·⋈· OF ·⋈·—

GAMES AND PASTIMES.

INVITATIONS.

Invitations should always be worded as concisely as possible. It is not necessary to conform to any strict rule with regard to wording, yet there are certain forms which through constant use have come to be looked upon as "proper."

Invitations to dine are usually worded as follows :

> *Mrs. Smith*
> *Requests the honor of*
> *Mr. Brown's company at dinner on*
> *Tuesday, the 11th January,*
> *at 7 o'clock.*
> *Jan. 3, 1887.*   *R. S. V. P.*

When "R. S. V. P." appears on the corner of an invitation, it is understood to mean that an answer is expected. In such cases it is proper to send an answer immediately, or at least as soon as possible, especially if the invitation be to dinner. The correct way of answering the above invitation is as follows :

```
Mr. Brown
Has the honor to accept
Mrs. Smith's
Kind invitation to Dinner
For Tuesday, the 11th January,
at 7 o'clock.
Jan. 3, '87
```

For receptions the wording is usually more brief. For example:

```
Mr. and Mrs. Jno. Smith,
Friday, July 12th,
From six till ten o'clock,
No. 417 Prairie Ave.
```

Parties admit of a greater variety of forms of invitations. The most common is:

```
Mrs. J. D. Williams
Requests the pleasure of your company
on
Thursday Evening, January 10th,
at 8 o'clock.
```

Or for a more informal affair:

```
Five o'clock tea,

Wednesday, March 20th.
```

Invitations to weddings are issued as coming from the parents of the bride. The following is generally the form:

> *Mr. and Mrs. D. M. Richardson*
> *Request the pleasure of your company at the*
> *marriage of their daughter*
> *ELOISE*
> *to*
> *DAVID H. MATSON,*
> *At their residence, 241 Vincennes Avenue,*
> *Thursday, May 14, 1886,*
> *at 8 o'clock.*

In preparing for your guests it is always well to devise some means of showing them that you have taken especial pains in their behalf, aside from the money you have spent. For instance, if your dinner be served by a caterer, a bouquet of flowers on the table which do not bear evidence of the florist's skill will, perhaps, be more appreciated than an elaborate floral design which is stamped "bought." Festooning or draping your reception rooms will have the same effect, the idea being to show your guests that you have thought enough of them to devote a portion of your time to arranging for their comfort and amusement.

DANCING.

At every social gathering where there is a piano or other musical instrument, and some one can be found willing and able to play, more or less dancing will be indulged in. In those cases the quadrilles, although the most enjoyable of all dances, are usually omitted because no one can be found who can "call." In order to remedy this difficulty wherever this book goes, we give a list of the most familiar square dances and the manner of calling them.

THE PLAIN QUADRILLE.

FIRST FIGURE.

First four :　　　Right and left..........................8 bars.
　　　　　　　　Balance................................8 bars.
　　　　　　　　Ladies' Chain..........................8 bars.
　　　　　　　　Balance ....4 bars.
　　　　　　　　Swing ....4 bars.
Side couples :　The same.
　　　　Repeat.

SECOND FIGURE.

First four:　　　Forward and back......................4 bars.
　　　　　　　　Forward again, ladies in the center.......4 bars.
　　　　　　　　Chassez all...........................4 bars.
　　　　　　　　Balance to Partners....................4 bars.
　　　　　　　　Swing................................4 bars.
Side couples :　The same.
　　　　Repeat.

THIRD FIGURE.

First four :　　　Forward and back ....4 bars.
　　　　　　　　First lady cross over....................4 bars.
　　　　　　　　Forward and back......................4 bars.
　　　　　　　　Ladies cross over......................4 bars.
　　　　　　　　Forward and back......................4 bars.
　　　　　　　　Forward again, four hands round.........8 bars.
　　　　　　　　Half right and left.....................4 bars.
Side couples :　The same.
　　　　Repeat.

FOURTH FIGURE.

First four :　　　Forward and back ....4 bars.
　　　　　　　　Cross over...........................4 bars.
　　　　　　　　Chassez to partners...................4 bars.
　　　　　　　　Cross back...........................4 bars.
　　　　　　　　Balance ....4 bars.
　　　　　　　　Swing...............................4 bars.
Side couples :　The same.
　　　　Repeat.

THE LANCIERS.

FIRST FIGURE.

First four : Forward and back......................4 bars.
Forward again and swing opposite partners.4 bars.
Ladies' chain back to partner ....4 bars.
Balance to corners.....................4 bars.
Swing...............................4 bars.

Side couples : The same.
Repeat.

SECOND FIGURE.

First four : Forward and back......................4 bars.
Forward again, ladies in the center.......4 bars.
Chassez to right and left................4 bars.
Swing partner to place.................4 bars.

All : All forward and back....................4 bars·
Swing partners.........................4 bars.

Side couples : The same.
Repeat.

THIRD FIGURE.

First four : Forward and back......................4 bars.
Forward again and salute. ....'4 bars.
Four ladies cross right hands, left to part-
ners................................4 bars.
Promenade half round.................4 bars.
Cross left hands and promenade back.....4 bars.

Side couples : The same.
Repeat.

FOURTH FIGURE.

First four : Lead to the right and salute ....4 bars.
Lead to the left and salute..............4 bars.
Balance to partners.....................4 bars.
Right and left........................4 bars.

Side couples : The same.
Repeat.

FIFTH FIGURE.

Grand right and left.....................16 bars.
First couple face out, side couples follow. 8 bars.
Chassez all............................ 8 bars.
March in single file................... 8 bars.
All forward and back.................. 4 bars.
Forward again and swing partners to
   place............................. 4 bars.

Repeat four times, each couple facing outward in succession.

AT THE CLOSE—Grand right and left half way round and promenade to seats.

WALTZ QUADRILLE.

FIRST FIGURE.

First four :	Right and left.......................	8 bars.
	Waltz	16 bars.
First four :	Ladies' Chain.........................	8 bars.
All :	Waltz.................................	16 bars.
Side four :	The same	

SECOND FIGURE.

First four :	Forward two..........................	16 bars.
All :	Waltz	16 bars.
	Repeat.	
Side four :	The same, twice.	

THIRD FIGURE.

First four :	Forward four.........................	4 bars.
	Forward again, change partners........	4 bars.
All :	Waltz.................................	16 bars.
	Repeat.	
Side four :	The same, twice.	

FOURTH FIGURE.

All :	Join hands, forward and back..........	4 bars.
	Turn partners to places...............	4 bars.
All :	Waltz.................................	16 bars.

This is done four times.

All :	Right and left half round.............. 8 bars.
All :	Waltz.................................16 bars.
Head couples :	Forward two ....16 bars.
All :	Waltz................................ ·6 bars.
Side couples :	The same.
All :	Waltz. At the close, salute............ 8 bars.

THE LOSS OF WAIST.

Women, especially those of the upper classes, who are not obliged to keep themselves in condition by work, lose after middle age (sometimes earlier) a considerable amount of their height, not by stooping, as men do, but by actual collapse, sinking down, mainly to be attributed to the perishing of the muscles that support the frame, in consequence of habitual and constant pressing of stays and dependence upon the artificial support by them afforded. Every girl who wears stays that press upon these muscles and restrict the free development of the fibres that support them, relieving them from their natural duties of supporting the spine, indeed incapacitating them from so doing, may feel sure that she is preparing herself to be a dumpy woman.

A great pity! exclaims *The London Lancet*. Failure of health among women when the vigor of youth passes away is but too patent, and but too commonly caused by this practice. Let the man that admires the piece of pipe that does duty for a human body picture to himself the wasted form and seamed skin. Most women, from long custom of wearing these stays, are really unaware how much they are hampered and restricted. A girl of 20, intended by nature to be one of her finest specimens, gravely assures one that her stays are not tight, being exactly the same size as those she was first put into, not perceiving her condemnation in the fact that she has grown five inches in height and two in shoulder-breadth. Her stays are not too tight, because the constant pressure has prevented the natural development of heart and lung space.

The dainty waist of the poets is [precisely that flexible slimness that is destroyed by stays. The form resulting from them is not slim, but a piece of pipe, and as inflexible. But, while endeavoring to make clear the outrage upon practical good sense and sense of beauty, it is necessary to understand and admit the whole state of the case. The reason, if not a necessity, for some sort of corset may be found when the form is very redundant; this, however, can not be with the very young and slight, but all that necessity could demand, and that practical good sense and fitness would concede, could be found in a strong elastic kind of jersey, sufficiently strong, and even stiff, under the bust to support it, and sufficiently elastic at the sides and back to injure no organs and impede no functions. Even in the case of the young and slight an elastic band under the false ribs would not be injurious, but, perhaps, the contrary, serving as a constant hint to keep the chest well forward and the shoulders back; but every stiff unyielding machine, crushing the ribs and destroying the fibre of muscle, will be fatal to health, to freedom of movement and beauty. It is scarcely too much to say that the wearing of such amounts to stupidity in those who do not know the consequences (for over and over again warning has been given), and to wickedness in those who do.

—Lady of the house:—So, Bridget, you think you will have to leave me, do you? Bridget—Yis, mum. Lady of the house—What is the trouble? Is the work too hard for you? Bridget—No, mum; I kin not complain about that. Lady of the house—Isn't the pay satisfactory? Bridget—Yis, mum. Lady of the house—What, then, is the trouble? Bridget—Yer see, mum, Oime a brunetter, an' that kitchen, mum, was fitted for a blonde. I'll not stay, mum, an' try my complexion, mum, day an' night.—*St. Paul Globe.*

—BETTER THAN A DOCTOR.—"I feel depressed to-night," remarked a large, down-town trunk manufacturer to his wife; "I think I have a touch of malaria." "I fancy it will soon pass away," replied the lady, without much concern. "Why don't you go around to the Grand Central station and watch them handle trunks for an hour. That will brighten you up."—*N. Y. Sun.*

—Algernon—Ya-as, deah boy, I've been desperwately ill; don't you know—desperwately. Fuller—Indeed; what was the trouble? Algernon—I had the b-bwain fever. Fuller, skeptically—O, what are you giving me?—*Rambler.*

—They call it a romantic marriage in Minnesota when a couple of the neighbors get the bride's father in a back room and sit on him to prevent his interrupting and breaking up the wedding.—*Ex.*

Ball's Health Preserving Corset.

Patented Feb. 22, 1881.

Kabo Boned; Pat. Oct. 19, 1886.

This Corset is in fact, what its name implies, when contrasted with the rigid, unyielding, "have to be broken in before worn". affairs of the present day. It is one of the snuggest, closest-fitting Corsets made, yet perfectly comfortable at all times, whether new or old, and needs no breaking in. Why? Because, by an ingenious arrangement of a fine coiled spring running back and forth across a section of the Corset (see cut above), which renders this section elastic, the Corset thereby conforms more closely to the figure, giving a finer outline. It also yields readily to every breath and movement of its wearer.

The elastic section is unlike rubber, in that it will not heat the person or decay with age, and emits no disagreeable odor. It is warranted to outwear the Corset unimpaired.

Made in white and drab satteen jean. Sizes from 18 to 36.

Testimony of Madame ADELINA PATTI, the "Queen of Song."

THE GRAND PACIFIC HOTEL, JOHN B. DRAKE & Co., Proprietors, CHICAGO, April 17, 1885.—*Dear Sirs:* I can understand physicians recommending "Ball's Corsets." I have tried them and regret not having known them before.

ADELINA PATTI.

To the Chicago Corset Co.

KABO

OUR NEW CORSET STIFFENING MATERIAL.

We have abondoned the use of French Horn in Ball's Corsets, and use instead a new material called **KABO,** *which, after being treated by a secret process, discovered by our Mr. Florsheim, is absolutely unbreakable.* **It will prevent the Corset from rolling up in wear.** *It is more pliable than horn, and does not break, nor become brittle and dry up while on the shelf. We warrant our Corsets boned with Kabo not to break or roll up in three months ordinary wear. We make a cheap grade of Corsets better than any imitations of Ball's Corsets, which we continue to bone with French Horn, and sell at less than any imitation offered to the trade, but we confidently recommend our Kabo boned Corset as the best and most durable of any Corset ever before offered to the trade. We have thoroughly tested Kabo by actual wear for over one year, and consequently offer the guarantee as herein stated.*

CHICAGO CORSET CO.

Testimony of Madame ADELINA PATTI, the "Queen
of Song.

The Grand Pacific Hotel

JNO. B. DRAKE & CO. PROPRIETORS,

Chicago 17 April 1885

Dear Sir,

I can understand physicians
recommending "Ball's Corsets"
I have tried them and regret not
having known them before

Adelina Patti

the Chicago Corset Co.

LAWN TENNIS.

The most popular of all out-door games, as well as the one requiring most skill, which can be participated in by ladies, is Lawn-Ten-
nis. It is not necessary to have a certain number of players, or that
the sexes be equally divided, since the game can be played by ladies
alone. Two, three or four ladies may have just as good an opportunity
of exercising their skill when alone as when accompanied by gentlemen.

A sketch on this game would be incomplete without some instructions for the ladies as to their mode of dress. Luckily, short dresses
are now the fashion and it is not necessary to have dresses made especially for the game. The player should get rid of all incumbrances or
anything which is likely to hinder her before the game begins. Ban-
gles and bracelets should be discarded, as well as rings, if the player
wear more than one. A large hat, especially one that is apt to come
loose and needs frequent adjustment, will be found uncomfortable,
Tight shoes should never be worn. The toes should be square or round.
and there should be no heels. An india-rubber sole is desirable, or one
with points (*i. e.*—small nails, whose heads protrude far enough to prevent slipping). In this connection corsets should not be forgotten, and
Ball's Kabo Corsets, which allow the utmost freedom of movement,
should be worn in preference to any other.

COURT AND IMPLEMENTS.

The court is 78 feet long. It is 27 feet wide for single game, and
36 feet for the double game. If no measuring chain be at hand, the
following will be found an easy way of marking out the court :

Provide yourself with two long measures ; select the place for the
net: then measure 36 feet across ; at each end put in a peg, and over each
peg slip the ring of a measure. On one measure take 39 feet, and on
the other 53 feet and ¾ inches ; pull both taut, and the place where the
two ends meet will be one corner of the court. Put in a peg, at 21 feet
from the net for the end of the service line. Next transpose the meas-

ures and repeat the same process. This will give the other corner of the court, and at 21 feet will be the other end of the service line, and one-half of your court is ready. Do the same on the other side of the net and you have your court complete. The side lines of the single court are made by marking off 4 feet, 6 inches, from each end of the base lines, and running lines parallel to the side-lines of the double court from one base-line to the other. Everything necessary is thus found except the central-line, which runs from the middle of one service-line to the middle of the other. The posts of the net stand 3 feet outside of the side-lines. If the court be intended for double play only, the inner side lines need not be carried farther from the net than the service lines. If a single court only is to be marked out, the diagonal is about 47 feet, 5 inches, instead of 53 feet, ¾ inches.

The net should be composed of cords not too thick to obstruct the view, while the meshes should be too small to allow a ball to pass through. It is well to bind the net at the top with a strip of duck or cotton, which can be seen in a bad light if the game be played at night.

Balls and rackets need no preliminary tinkering, although the player should exercise great care in the purchase of a racket. Do not get an odd-shaped racket. The simplest form, strung in the usual way, with an octagonal handle, will be found the best. It should not be heavier than 14 or 14½ ounces.

DEFINITION OF TERMS.

SERVICE.—By service is meant the first toss of the ball by the person who starts the game.

FIRST STROKE.—By this is meant the return of the service.

STROKE.—By this is meant the return of a ball after it has struck the ground.

VOLLEY.—A ball is volleyed when it is returned before it reaches the ground.

HALF-VOLLEY.—This stroke consists in taking the ball just as it begins to rise after striking the ground.

LOB.—A lob is a ball tossed in the air so that it shall fall far back in the court, and shall be out of reach of a player standing as far forward as the service-line.

BISQUE.—A bisque is one stroke given in each set of a match, either by itself or to increase or diminish the odds. In other words, a player to whom a bisque is given can at any time in the set add one stroke to his score simply by claiming it.

RULES.

SINGLE HANDED GAME.

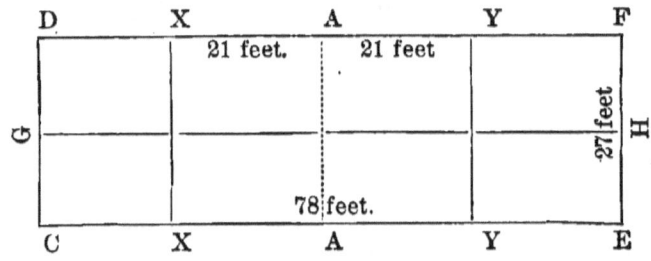

AA—Net.
CD–EF—Base lines.
CE–DF—Side lines.
GH—Half court line.
XX–YY—Service lines.

1.   The players shall stand on opposite sides of the net; the player who first delivers the ball shall be called the *server*, the other the *striker-out*. At the end of the first game the server becomes the striker-out, and the striker-out becomes the server, and so on alternately in the subsequent games.

2.   The server serves with one foot on the base-line, and the other behind that line, but not necessarily upon the ground.   Service must be delivered from the right and left courts alternately, beginning from the right.

3.   The ball served must drop within the service line, half court line, and side line of the court diagonally opposite to that from which it was served, or upon any such line.

4.   It is a *fault* if the service is delivered from the wrong court, or if the server does not stand as directed above, or if the ball served drops in the net or beyond the service line, or if it drops out of court or in the wrong court.

5.   A fault may not be taken.   It cannot be claimed after the next service has been delivered.

No. 6.   After a fault the server shall serve again from the same court from which he served that fault, unless it was a fault because served from the wrong court.

7. The service must not be volleyed.

8. The server must not serve until the striker-out is ready. If the latter attempts to return the service he is deemed ready. Neither a service nor fault is counted when the striker-out is not ready.

9. A ball is in play from the moment at which it is delivered in service until one of the players loses a stroke.

10. The return of a service may be good, even though the ball touch the net, but a service, although otherwise good, is a fault if the ball touch the net.

11. Either player loses a stroke if the ball in play touch him or anything he wears or carries, except his racket in the act of striking; or if he touch or strike the ball in play with his racket more than once; or if he touch the net or any of its supports while the ball is in play; or if he volley the ball before it has passed the net.

12. The server wins a stroke if the striker-out volley the service or fail to return the service, or the ball in play, or return the service or the ball in play so that it drops outside any of the lines which bound his opponent's court, or otherwise lose a stroke as provided above.

13. The striker-out wins a stroke if the server serve two consecutive faults, or fail to return the ball in play so that it drops outside any of the lines which bound his opponent's court, or otherwise lose a stroke as provided above.

14. The players should change sides, either after every set or after every game, whichever they prefer.

SCORING.

15. On either player winning his first stroke, the score is called 15 for that player ; on either player winning his second stroke, the score is called 30 for that player ; on either player winning his third stroke, the score is called 40 for that player ; and the fourth stroke won by either player, is scored game for that player, except as below :

If both players have won three strokes the score is called deuce ; and the next stroke won by either player is scored advantage for that player. If the same player wins the next stroke he wins the game; if he lose the next stroke, the game is again called deuce ; and so on until either player win the two strokes immediately following the score of deuce, when the game is scored for that player.

The player who wins six games first wins the set, except as below:

If both players win five games the score is called games-all; and the next game won by either player is scored advantage game for that player. If the same player win the next game, he wins the set ; if he lose, the score is again called games-all, and so on until one of the players wins two games immediately following the score of games-all, when he wins the set.

Players may agree not to play advantage-sets, but to decide the set by one game after arriving at the score of games-all.

ODDS.

16. A bisque may be claimed by the receiver of the odds at any time during a set, except as below:

A bisque can not be taken after the service has been delivered.

The server cannot take a bisque after a fault, but the striker-out may do so.

One or more bisques may be given in augmentation or diminution of other odds.

Half-fifteen is one stroke given at the beginning of the second and every subsequent alternate game of a set.

Fifteen is one stroke given at the beginning of every game of a set.

Half-Thirty is one stroke given at the beginning of the first game; two strokes at the beginning of the second game; and so on alternately, in all the subsequent games of a set.

Thirty is two strokes given at the beginning of every game of a set.

Half-forty is two strokes given at the beginning of the first game; three strokes at the beginning of the second game ; and so on, alternately in all the subsequent games of a set.

Forty is three strokes given at the beginning of every game of a set.

Half Court: The players having agreed into which court the giver of the odds shall play, the latter loses a stroke if the ball, returned by him, drop outside any of the lines which bound that court.

THREE-HANDED AND FOUR-HANDED GAMES.

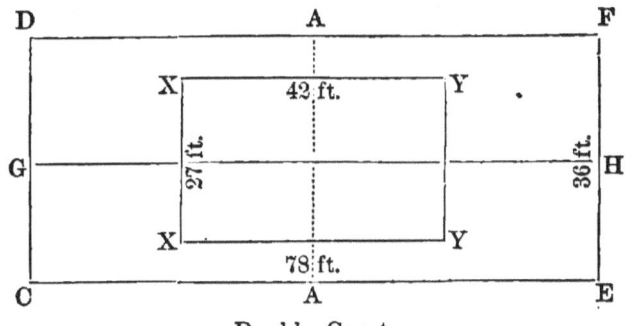

Double Court.

NOTE.—The double court is similar to the single court, except that the service lines are not drawn beyond the points X X and Y Y.

1. In the three-handed game the simple player shall serve in every alternate game.

2. In the four-handed game the pairs may decide which partner shall serve and strike out first. The partner of the player who served in the first game shall serve in the third, and the partner of the player who served in the second game shall serve in the fourth, and so on.

3. The players shall take the service alternately throughout each game; no player shall receive or return a service delivered to his partner; and the order of service and of striking out shall not be changed for the set.

4. The ball served must drop within the service-line, half-court-line, and service-side-line of the court diagonally opposite to the one from which it is served, or upon any such line. If it does not drop in this way it is a *fault*.

—Young clerk to his employer—"Sir, there's a lady wishes to speak to you." Employer—"Good looking?" Clerk—"Yes, sir." Employer, on returning to the office—"A nice judge of beauty you are, I must say." Clerk—"You see, sir, I didn't know but what the lady might be your wife." Employer—"So she is."—*Troy Times.*

—The season is over, thank heaven, when the weak young man at the picnic puts on a girl's hat and tries to be funny.—*Puck.*

STYLE B.

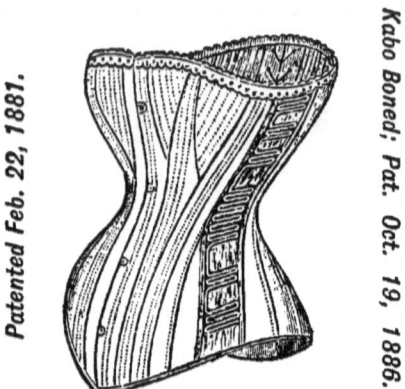

Patented Feb. 22, 1881.

Kabo Boned; Pat. Oct. 19, 1886.

This Corset is made in the same style as our "Health Preserving," and is a very popular Corset. It fits perfectly, and gives a graceful figure to the wearer.

Made in white and drab satteen jean, in sizes from 18 to 36.

Testimony of Mrs. PARRY, of the "Mapleson Opera Company."

PALMER HOUSE, CHICAGO, April 18, 1885.

To CHICAGO CORSET CO.

I fully recommend Ball's Corsets as being best adapted to singers, or, in fact, any one wishing to have a comfortable Corset.

MRS. J. PARRY,
Mapleson Opera Co.

Testimony of Madame EMMA STEINBACH, the famous Alto.

PALMER HOUSE.

Chicago, 18 April 1889.

Sehr geehrte Herren!

Meinen besten Dank für das wirklich ganz ausgezeichnete und bequeme Corset, [illegible] [illegible] sehr schön gearbeitet ist.

Ergebenst

Emma Steinbach

(TRANSLATION.)

My Dear Sirs:—My best thanks for your excellent and comfortable Corset. It is a beauty of Workmanship.

Yours, EMMA STEINBACH.

PARLOR GAMES.

HOW TO MAKE MONEY WITHOUT WORK.

Draw a number of lines from a common point in the manner of radii of a circle. Then ask each participant to place a coin upon one of the lines and to watch it carefully, taking care to remember which was his line and which was his money. Then move the money about on the lines until none of the coins are in their original places. Then, pointing to their lines, ask one after another: "Is this your line?" The answer in each case will, of course, be "Yes." Then point to the coins on the lines and ask them successively: "Is this your money?" And the answer will be "No" in every instance. Then pretend you are about to pocket the money, with the remark: "Well, as nobody seems to own this money, I'll keep it myself."

HARMLESS GAMBLING.

Each one deposits a small sum in a pool. Then put a complete pack of cards into a bag and shake up well. The party forms a circle and the bag is handed around, each one drawing three cards. Those drawing pairs will be blessed by some good fortune in the near future and recover the sum deposited by them. The King of Hearts is the God of Love, and draws double the amount deposited; if a lady has drawn him she will soon be united with one who will be true to her forever. The Queen of Hearts is Cupid, and if drawn by a gentleman gives him the same good fortune as the King gives the lady. If any one draws both King and Queen he clears the pool, and will never know what misfortune is. Fives and nines are unlucky numbers, and the drawers must deposit an additional stake besides the regular one paid by all at the opening of each new game. Three knaves drawn by a lady shows she will be married three times; three sevens, that she will be an old maid; three fives, that she will be a grass widow.

MESMERISM.

This should be practiced only upon persons of a good natured disposition.

Take two plates with a glass full of water on each. Blacken the bottom of one of the plates over a candle or kerosene lamp and hand the blackened plate with the glass of water to the victim. Then proceed to tell the audience that the operation about to be performed is a severe strain on the nerves and beseech them to remain perfectly quiet, to say nothing and above all, not to laugh. Having done this you take the other plate in your hand and instruct the victim to loook straight into your eyes and to go through the same operations you do, all the while watching you closely. You then dip two fingers into the water and wipe them across your forehead ; next you draw your forefinger across the bottom of the plate, and, starting from the top of the forehead, draw it down to the end of the nose, the victim doing the same and of course leaving a streak of lamp-black on his face. After you have adorned him with moustaches, double eyebrows, chin whiskers and several spots of war paint, tell him he is mesmerized and have him look in the glass. If the trick has been well performed, it may indeed be called mesmerism.

PINNING A THIMBLEFUL OF WATER ON THE WALL.

Fill a thimble with water and take a pin, ostensibly for the purpose of pinning the thimble to the wall. Ask for the assistance of some good natured young gentleman, who will immediately undertake to help you. When you reach the wall drop the pin accidentally. Of course the young gentleman has to bend very low to reach the pin. While he is in that position, empty the water from the thimble upon his head or down his back, and the trick is performed.

HOW TO PLACE AN EGG SO THAT IT CAN NOT BE BROKEN WITH A DISH PAN.

Bring in an egg and a dish pan, and let every one examine them to convince the audience that there is no fraud connected with them. Then announce that you are about to lay the egg upon the floor where no one will be able to smash it with the dish pan. Place the egg in a corner of the room, and it will not be possible to reach it with the dish pan.

THE DWARF.

The articles required for this are always at the disposal of every-one. They consist of a pair of boots, a hat, a cloak or shawl, and a table which can be draped in such a way that the audience cannot look through beneath. It requires two persons to perform the act. One of them places his hands into the boots and rests them upon the table. This person forms the feet, body and head of the dwarf, the second person being required only for the hands. The latter stands behind the first in such a way that when the cloak is thrown over both he is entirely concealed, with the exception of his hands, which he stretches forward, one on each side of the person before him, so as to make them appear to be the hands of what seems to be a little man standing on the table.

The cloak or shawl is then thrown about the dwarf and he is ready to amaze the audience with his eccentricities. His hands and feet of course do not act in harmony, but the effect is enhanced bv that fact.

MIND READING.

Have each participant write a short sentence or a word on a slip of paper and fold it up, and collect the slips in a hat. Then, drawing the slips from the hat, one after another, you hold each one of them above your head, unfold it, and, pressing it against your forehead, you say what it contains. If well performed this trick often causes a great deal of astonishment, no one being able to understand how you have learned the contents of the paper. The manner of doing it consists in invent-ing a sentence for the first one, and then, as you lay it down, obtaining a quick glance at the writing on it; then you repeat what was on the first slip as coming from the second, and so on until you have reached the last, when you must manage to get rid of that by putting it into your pocket unobserved, or crunching it up and throwing it away.

APPLE-EATING MATCH.

Suspend two or more apples from a chandelier or a fastening in the ceiling, and then offer a prize to the participant who first finishes eating his apple with his hands tied to his back. It is well to offer a prize of some value in this instance, because few will be found to face the roars of laughter which will greet their attempts to bite into the apples without the hope of a substantial reward.

THE BROOM-HANDLE GIANT.

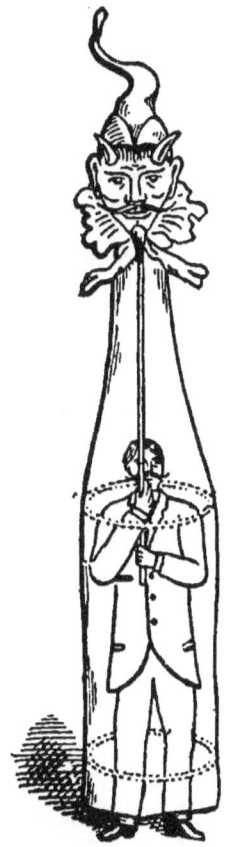

A glance at the illustration herewith given will be sufficient for most persons who desire to appear in this mirth-provoking costume. Secure a large, grotesque head and fasten it to a broom-handle. Then drape the figure with coarse cloth, which can be seen through. A hoop should be placed about the shoulders and another about the knees, fastened securely to the skirt. The lower hoop should be fastened to the waist by tapes in such a way as to prevent the skirt from reaching the ground, however much the giant contracts. No one realizes, until he has seen it tried, how much fun can be had by masquerading in this costume. You can enter as a dwarf in a crouching position; then begin to draw yourself up to your full height; then raise the stick gradually until the head reaches the ceiling; then make a graceful bow to the audience, which by this time will be convulsed in laughter; then proceed to amuse them by antics which cannot fail to be laughable, even if performed by a person usually grave and sedate.

THE YOUNG GIANT.

Another species of giant, not quite so popular as the broom-handle giant is the YOUNG GIANT. It requires two persons to make him.

A light boy is placed upon the shoulders of one of the tallest men n the assembly. His (the boy's) legs are held firmly against the sides of he man under the latter's arm pits, while the man's hands are held gainst the breast. A long coat, cloak or shawl is then placed around he boy completely concealing the legs of the boy and arms and head f the man. A peep hole should be left in the cloak somewhere so that he lower part of the giant can see before him. The most striking haracteristic of this giant is his youthful appearance, which is not at ll in keeping with his size.

SOME HARD LINES TO REPEAT.

Following are a few stanzas from which a great deal of amusement can be drawn, by asking persons unused to them to repeat one of them several times in succession rapidly :

A Big Black Bug bit a Big Black Bear.

Peter Piper picked a peck of prickly pepper,
A peck of prickly pepper Peter Piper picked ;
Now, if Peter Piper picked a peck of prickly pepper,
Produce the peck of prickly pepper, that Peter Piper picked.

As I went into the garden I saw five brave maids,
Sitting on five broad beds, braiding broad braids ;
I said to the five brave maids, sitting on five broad beds,
Braiding broad braids, "Braid broad braids, brave maids."

It sometimes astonishes a party to learn that :

Inmudeelis,
Inclaynoneis.
Infirtaris,
Inoaknoneis.

Translated into plain English, is no more than :

In mud eel is,
In clay none is.
In fir tar is,
In oak none is.

DRAWING EXTRAORDINARY.

Provide each person with a pencil and a blank sheet of paper. Then decide upon something to be drawn with closed eyes. A pig is a good thing to begin with. When the pictures are done the results will be curious. Some pigs will be standing on their own heads, others will have their tails in their mouths, and some will have all their legs on one end of their bodies

GROTESQUE SHADOW PANTOMIMES.

A screen of muslin or other white cloth should be spread across the room. A room with sliding doors can be readily arranged for this purpose. A lamp is then placed on the floor with a reflector back of it. When you stand before the light your image will be reflected upon the screen and magnified to immense proportions. By jumping over the lamp it appears to those on the other side that you have jumped up through the ceiling. It is glorious fun if performed by persons who have studied the matter a little. Pouring sawdust from a vessel presents the appearance of a liquid. Razors, shears, and such articles appear ludicrously large; a scrap of paper placed on each ear arouses shouts of laughter, while a wad of paper placed upon the nose suggests a tremendous wart. Some mirth-provoking scenes can easily be devised.

PLAYING BLIND MAN.

An assembly can soon be made to realize how important their sight is to them by a few games like the following :

Have them all stand on one side of the room. Then mark a spot on the opposite wall and request them to close their eyes and advance toward it, and indicate with their index finger where the spot is. The chances are that no one will come near it.

Place a gentleman within a few yards of a table on which stands a lighted candle. Securely blindfold him and have him turn completely around three or four times. Then bid him advance toward the table and blow out the candle. He does not dare to get within range for fear of burning his nose and will make frantic efforts to blow it out when standing at right angles with it.

Bring in a high silk hat and let every one look at it carefully. Then bid them close their eyes and indicate on the wall how high the crown would reach if the hat were placed on the floor. Some would appear to think a silk hat is a veritable " Stove pipe."

THE CUSHION DANCE.

A hassock is placed end upwards in the middle of the floor, round which the players form a circle, with hands joined, having first divided themselves into two parties of equal number.

The adversaries, facing each other, begin business by dancing round the hassock a few times; then suddenly one side tries to pull the other forward, so as to force one of their number to touch the hassock and to upset it. The struggle that necessarily ensues is a source of great fun, causing as much or even more merriment to spectators of the scene than to the players themselves. At last, in spite of the utmost dexterity, down goes the hassock or cushion; some one's foot is sure to touch it before long, when the unfortunate individual is dismissed from the circle and compelled to pay a forfeit.

The advantage that the gentlemen have over the ladies in this game is very great; they can leap over the stool and avoid it times without number, while the ladies are continually impeded by their dresses. It generally happens that two gentlemen are left to keep up the struggle, which in most cases is a very prolonged one.

THE GAME OF GEOGRAPHY.

In this game the party is divided into two sides and each has a leader. The leader of one side starts the game by selecting a letter from the alphabet, and calling out, for example, "Rivers," when the leader of the opposite side mentions the name of a river beginning with the letter selected, and is followed in rapid succession by the one next to him. If any one makes a mistake giving a lake instead of a river, he must take his seat. If any one hesitates, the opposite leader counts ten rapidly, and if the word is not forthcoming, the participant who is passed must be seated. If each one in the line answers correctly, the side scores. The other side is then put to the test and the game continued until one side has scored 5, or has downed all the members of the opposite side.

CONSEQUENCES.

This game has been in vogue for a long time, yet many ways may be contrived of playing it, so as to make it appear new each time. One of the favorite ways of playing it is as follows: The leader of the game provides each of the players with a pencil and a slip of paper. He then requests them to write at the head of the slip *one or more adjectives*, and to fold over the top of the slip so as to conceal the writing. Each one of them passes his slip to his neighbor on the left, and proceeds to write on the new slip handed to him by his neighbor on the right; (2) *a gentleman's name*, again folding, and proceeding as before with (3) *one or more adjectives;* (4) *a lady's name;* (5) *some locality;* (6) *an article of lady's wear;* (7) *something one is apt to do when in love;* (8) *what he said;* (9) *what she said;* (10) *what the end of it was.*

Then the leader collects the papers and proceeds to edify the audience with intelligence something like this :

The (1) *brilliant, bombastic* (2) *John Smith* called on the (3) *emaciated* (4) *Mary Ann Boggs*, who resides (5) *down in Bridgeport*. He found her attired in a (6) *Ball's Corset*, and immediately proceeded to (7) *hug* her. He said to her, (8) " *Why should the spirit of mortal be proud?* " and she answered (9) " *tootsey-wootsey.*" The end of it was (10) *a family row.*

THE COMIC CONCERT.

In this performance the company for the time imagine themselves a band of musicians. Each provides himself, or herself, with a musical instrument of some kind, or an article which bears a resemblance to a musical instrument. Not only can all the violins, harps, flutes, accordeons, pianos or jewsharps in the house be made use of, but such things as funnels, dish pans, or pot covers may be brought into requisition. These instruments are all to be performed upon, at the same time, each one imitating with his voice or by some other means the real sound of the instrument he is burlesqueing. The leader begins playing some familiar air on his imaginary violincello, or whatever else it may be, imitating a musician as well as he can, both in action and voice.

The others follow. The sight, as may well be imagined, is exceedingly ludicrous and the noise deafening. Suddenly the leader, without any warning, gives away his instrument, and snatches that of some one else, substituting, for his former antics, the ones proper for his new instrument. The performer who has been deprived of his instrument seizes that of some one else, the music in the meanwhile continuing. Every one is expected to watch the leader, and to make a sudden change when he does. The game may be continued for some time, each change creating new sights and sounds that are always laughable.

SOME HARD BLOWING.

Secure a hair from some lady's head and with a tiny bit of shoe-maker's wax fasten it to a small piece of paper about an inch square, curled up in such shape that it could be readily blown away if not fastened. Place this in the middle of the table and stand a tumbler on the other end of the hair. Then announce that the tumbler standing before this piece of paper so intercepts the current of air that it is impossible to blow it (the paper) away. This trick causes a great deal of surprise if the hair is not detected, no one being able to understand how it is that the paper flutters but does not fly off.

THE GREAT HEAD.

Enter the room with an air of great concern, and, in a voice of alarm, tell the assembly that you have just come from the kitchen, and that, through the door leading to the pantry, you had caught sight of an enormous head; that you are sure it is not the head of a human being, and that you have never seen an animal with such a head; and proceed to arouse their curiosity and alarm, warning them not to venture down alone, but to go in a body, armed with such weapons as are handy. When the party reaches the pantry door, open it and disclose an enormous head of cabbage.

FORTUNE-TELLING WITH A BIBLE.

Insert a large key into a bible so that it shall touch the verse beginning with, "Set me as a seal upon thine arm, as a seal upon thy heart." Tie the key in place very firmly so that it will not slip. Then have a lady and gentlemen hold the bible by the key with their right fore-fingers. The bible will be balanced in such a way that it can turn when necessary. Then the person who desires to know whom he or she is going to marry (one of the two holding the bible) begins with the letter a and goes through the alphabet, the verse being repeated after each letter When the initial of the surname of the person whom they are seeking is reached, the bible will turn towards the finger of the lucky holder of the bible, and a guess will reveal the full name. The most important of all the things required to work the charm is absolute faith, without which it will not work.

MISPLACED OBJECTS.

Let each one be provided with a piece of paper and a pencil, and write a list of half a dozen or more names of objects. It makes no difference what the names are, and they may be embellished with adjectives. Then the leader takes some familiar poem or prose selection and begins to read, every now and then stopping before a noun, which must be supplied by the person whose turn it is to read a name. Thus:

" Friends, Romans, countrymen, lend me your —"
" Fresh fish."
" I come to bury —"
" Diamonds."
" Not to praise him.
" The evil that men do lives after them.
" The good is oft interred with their—"
" Shaving mug."
In this manner the game continues.

APPRENTICES.

This game is often a very merry one. It can be played with or without forfeits. It is commenced by one of the ladies declaring that she has had so much trouble with her son that she found it necessary to apprentice him to some artisan, and that the first thing he did was to make some article of which she gives only the initials, and the next person must guess what the article was. Then she in turn tells of her woes with her boy and how she had to apprentice him to some other artisan, and so the game is continued. The following will serve for an illustration:

" Since my boy has left school he has been doing nothing but quar reling with my neighbors' boys. He came home with so many black eyes that I found it necessary to apprentice him to a butcher, who could supply him with beefsteak for them. The first thing he did was to sell a M. C."

" *Mutton chop.* My boy has also been the cause of much trouble in our neighborhood by throwing stones. So I apprenticed him to a stone-cutter. He at once made a G. S."

" *Grave stone.* My boy wore out so many shoes that I sent him to a cobbler to be taught shoemaking. The first day a lady called who wanted some shoes, and he made her some M's,"

" M's—what can they be? Surely not mis-fits? Oh, mocassins "—
and so the game is continued.

The fun comes in when somebody makes a ridiculous answer.

A NEW FORM OF BELL.

Tie a piece of cord around the handle of a poker leaving the two
ends each about a foot long. Take the ends of the cord and pass them
around the balls of the thumbs so that you can lift the poker in your
hands. Then put the ends of the cords into the ears, pressing them in
with your thumbs. If the poker is now struck by some one the sound
will appear very loud to you though scarcely audible to any one else.
A sharp blow from a hard substance will sound like a deep note from a
piano. If a hammer is used the sound will resemble a church-bell. If
the poker is a large one the tremendous sound it appears to produce
will be a matter of great surprise to any one who tries the experiment.

A CHESTNUT COURT.

The game is started by one of the party giving utterance to a very
old joke. Then everybody groans, and some one opens court to try the
culprit for his offense. A jury is chosen, and they decide upon the
punishment to be meted out. This may be that he must listen to five
puns from some one who is alleged to be a punster, and must laugh at
every one of them; or it may be that every one in the company should
tell him a funny story, or some other punishment may be inflicted upon
him which will afford amusement for all concerned. If he successfully withstands all this, he is permitted to state which of the jokes he
has heard is the worst, and the person who perpetrated the latter must
take his place. Thus the game continues.

THE BLIND SLAVES.

If the party is a large one ask five young gentlemen (bachelors of
course) if they desire to impersonate blind slaves and will allow themselves to be dressed for that purpose. When you have the five victims,
ask four ladies to assist you in the preparations.

You then seat the gentlemen in a row behind some sliding doors
and securely blindfold them. Next you require them to make fists of

their right hands and rest them on their left elbows in an easy and restful position. Then, with a bit of charcoal, draw eyes nose and mouth on the back of each fist. When this is done, dress the right arm of each gentleman with white aprons, tiny shawls, napkins and articles of that description in such a way as to make it appear to be a very small infant, the fist being the head, and having a hood around it. When the doors are thrown open the scene of five bachelors tenderly holding five babes will be greeted with roars of laughter. When these have somewhat subsided remove the bandages from the eyes of the blind slaves. Their astonishment will be immense, and hardly less ludicrous than their former innocence.

EARTH FIRE AND WATER.

The game is started by one of the company tossing a ball to another calling out one of the three words "earth," "air" or "water," and the person catching the ball must call out the name of some animal inhabiting the element called before the ball reaches his or her hand. For instance, if "air" be called, the person to whom the ball is thrown must call out "eagle," "hawk," or "butterfly" or other bird, before the ball lands, or pay a forfeit. "Fire" may be called, in which case the person catching the ball must remain silent.

FORFEITS.

A list of some ways of redeeming them, which may be found handy:

1. Kneel to the wittiest, bow to the prettiest, and kiss the one you love best.

2. Take (here mention the name of the stoutest lady present) up stairs and bring her down on a feather. [He brings down the word "her," written on a slip of paper, bearing it on a feather.]

3. Say five flattering things to some one, using the letter l in each. (Other letters may be substituted.)

4. Keep a serious face for two minutes, no matter what the rest of the company does.

5. Stand upon a handkerchief with one of the opposite sex without touching each other. (This disposes of two forfeits at once, and is done in this manner: A handkerchief is placed underneath the door, and one stands on each side of the door.)

6. Play the Dumb Orator. (This is done by reciting inwardly some selection, and making all the necessary gestures, but letting no sound escape your lips.)

7. Pose as a statue in the way desired by each. (The poser must mount a box and stand in the different positions required by the rest, each one devising some new position.)

8. Repeat five times rapidly: "Willy Wite and wife went a voyage to Winsor and West Wickham one Witsun Wednesday.

9. Stand in the middle of the room and make a very woeful face for one minute.

10. Kiss yourself in the looking glass.

11. Count twenty-five backwards, at the same time holding a book and turning the leaves from one to twenty-five as you count.

12. Imitate without laughing the voices of five animals which your companions name.

13. The one who pays the forfeit stands with her back to another who makes signs indicating a kiss, a pinch, and a cuff on the ear, and when the former is asked which is wanted, the first, second or third, whatever is chosen must be given.

14. When forfeits have become tiresome all the balance may be redeemed at once by requiring the balance to perform a cat's concert:— All singing at once, as if in chorus, but each singing a different song.

THE VICTIMS OF CORSETS.

" There is no article of underwear that women are so particular and fussy about as a corset," said the forewoman in the corset department of a fashionable store. "And really there is no other that they have a better right to be particular about, for a nice, easy, good-fitting corset is a joy forever, and the reverse is enough to try the temper of a saint."

" What do you think of the effect of corset-wearing on the health?" asked the reporter.

" Corsets, when worn sensibly, are certainly a great convenience and comfort. Indeed, there are but few ladies who know how to get along without them in some form or shape. There are, to be sure, some ladies who do not wear corsets, and never have worn them; but I think this is often quite as much affectation on their part as on the part of others who, through ignorance and vanity, are addicted to tight lacing. At all events, I don't see how a stylish woman could once know the real support afforded by an easy but perfectly fitting pair of stays, and then relinquish them willingly. With stout women especially corsets are a great comfort. They render one insensible to the skirt-bands, which otherwise cut into the flesh. They tend to brace up the bust, support and gird up the waist all round from the arm-pits to the hips, and down over the hips, and by the busk, or corset-board, to hold down and shield the embonpoint. But then fleshy women are naturally more tempted to tight lacing than any others, so that, after all, those whom sensible corsets are most apt to benefit are just the ones most likely to suffer from an abuse of the system. Tight lacing, however, is fast disappearing, in this country at least, and is due very largely to the new departure in corset making as shown in Ball's Corset, which, by its coiled spring elastic section, enables the wearer to obtain the most perfect fitting corset imaginable, and yet be entirely free from the harmful pressure of the rigid corset, and, in my opinion, needs only a trial to be worn by every lady in our land."

"Does not the whalebone or French horn used in corsets generally break before corsets are worn any length of time?"

"Yes," replied the forewoman, "that has always been the complaint, but that has been obviated by the new boning material, called KABO, used by the Chicago Corset Co. in the manufacture of Ball's Corsets. The Kabo does not break or roll up in wear, and in consequence the corsets give better satisfaction and last longer than those boned with any other material."

THE ANTIQUITY OF THE CORSET.

As long ago as the days of the Greeks and Romans, a slight *elancee* figure was admired, and stoutness looked upon as a deformity. Martial ridiculed fat women, and Ovid put large waists in the first rank of his remedies against love. Several remedies were tried then as now, not only to restrain an expanding figure, but to enhance the beauties of a very slight one. But they were of a different kind from those with which we are familiar. Bandages were worn with the generic name of *fasciae mamillares*. These consisted of the *strophium*, the cloth worn around the bosom, the *tenia*, a simple band below, and the *zona*, or waist-belt. When bandages failed, those who valued the beauty of their figures had recourse to a remedy prescribed by Serenus Sammonicus. They enveloped their busts with garlands of ivy, which were thrown on the fire as soon as withdrawn, and afterward rubbed all the upper part of their figures either with goose fat mixed with warm milk or with an egg of a partridge. Men were as vain as the women, if we are to believe Aristophanes and other writers. The great comic dramatist mocked his contemporary Cinesas for wearing busks of lindenwood; and Capitolinus, in his biography of the Emperor Anthony, mentions that he also had recourse to them to compress his swelling figure. Testimony is conflicting, however. Some contend that the ancients wore veritable corsets, arguing that when Homer, in describing Juno's toilet when she wishes to captivate Jupiter, speaks of the two girdles worn around her waist—the one bordered with gold fringe, the other borrowed from Venus—he was really describing a Greek corset, and that the egide or cuirass of Minerva which Virgil describes is to be interpreted in the same manner. But this view is surely mistaken, for no monument of antiquity, no artistic work, no evidence gleaned from other sources, point to the use of stiff, unyielding whalebone corsets.—*London World.*

TIGHT LACING.

An inquest was recently held on the body of a widow at Paddington, England. Owing to tight lacing the stomach had become so contracted at the centre as to present the appearance of an upper and lower one. Death had been caused by syncope. The Coroner stated that four or five other deaths recently investigated had been caused by tight lacing.

Tell a person to think of a number, for instance 6; multiply by 3, 18; add 1, 19; multiply by 3, 57; add to this the number thought of, 63. Then tell you what is the number produced; it will always end with 3. Strke off the 3, and you know that he thought of 6.

A school teacher being asked how many pupils he had, answered: "One-half study mathematics, one-fourth natural philosophy, one-seventh preserve silence, and there are three females besides." From this answer the number of his pupils can be ascertained—28.

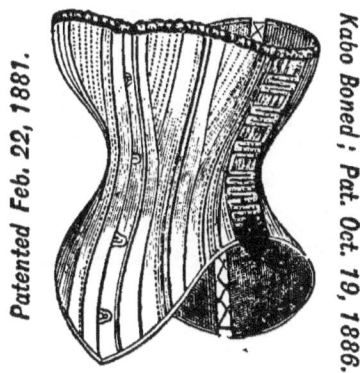

Patented Feb. 22, 1881.

Kabo Boned ; Pat. Oct. 19, 1886.

This Corset possesses the same coiled spring elastic side sections as our Health Preserving Corset No. 1, and is more desirable for those ladies who prefer a short Corset under the arms, it being cut away from over the hips, as shown in the above cut. Ladies who, for any reason, prefer this pattern of Corset, will find this the best and most satisfactory one in the market.

Made in white and drab satteen jean.   Sizes 18 to 36.

Testimony of Madame EMMA STEINBACH, the Famous Alto.

PALMER HOUSE, CHICAGO, April 18, 1885.

My Dear Sirs : My best thanks for your excellent and comfortable Corset. It is a beauty of workmanship.   Yours,

EMMA STEINBACH.

Testimony of Madame ROSINA CARACCIOLO, of the Mapleson Opera Co.

.THE GRAND PACIFIC HOTEL, JOHN B. DRAKE & Co., Proprietors, CHICAGO, April 18, 1885.—*Gentlemen :* My gratitude and testimonial of satisfaction for your Corset. It is a pleasure for me to state that it is excellent, especially for its close fitting without discomfort, at the same time permitting the natural movements of the body. I recommend it to all, and remain, very truly yours,

Mme. ROSINA CARACCIOLO.

Testimony of Madame FURSCH-MADI, the Prima Donna.

The Grand Pacific Hotel

JNO B. DRAKE & CO. PROPRIETORS,

Chicago, April 18 1885

Dear Sir.

After having
tried Balls Corsets
I find them in
quality superior to
any I have used
before. I heartily
recommend them to
the public

E. Fursch-Madi

DIALOGUES.

KABO.

CHARACTERS

John Spofford, a crusty old man.
Blackburne Snoggs, a penniless lawyer.
Henry Ayres, a young gentleman.
Virginia Almira Spofford, a spinster with a small fortune, sister of John Spofford.
Jeannette Spofford, daughter of John Spofford.

Note.—Snoggs and Virginia should not be burlesqued, but should be acted as comedy characters.

SCENE: A room in Spofford's house. As the curtain rises Virginia and Jeannette are discovered sewing and talking over their work.

Vir.—Yes, Nettie, I have traveled far and seen much, but have never discovered so obstreperous an animal as an Alpine mule. The one I rode frightened me more than any thing has done since I was in my teens.

Jean. (slyly)—That was a *long* time ago.

Vir.—Oh, yes, indeed, laugh at me for saying so, but you should try to ride him ! His owner called him Kabo.

Jean.—Kabo ! What a curious name. Why did he call him so ?

Vir.—He says he calls him Kabo because it is impossible to break him, you cannot wear him out, and he makes a good *stay* whenever he chooses. I soon discovered that he was right. That animal preferred the brink of a precipice to a broad path every time. He would make such sharp turns that I nearly fell from his back a dozen times while we were upon the mountain, and when we came down he was so anxious to get home that he determined to get rid of his rider, and sent me flying over his head. I landed in the lake !

Jean.—Landed !

Vir.—No ; not exactly landed, because I went down, and had it not been for Snoggs——

Jean.—I see ; he pulled you out. But how did Snoggs happen to be in Switzerland ? I thought he did not have enough money to support him here.

Vir.—That was before his aunt rejected him. He is in want now, but, though poor, he is a gentleman still. (Puts her hand to her heart and sighs.)

Enter SNOGGS.

Jean.—Here he is. Mr. Snoggs, we were just speaking of you.

Snoggs—Thank you. (Sighs.)

Jean.—Why do you sigh ?

Snoggs—I was thinking that before my elbows stuck out of my coat many ladies, Miss Jeannette, sometimes thought of me. But now— (He glances ruefully at the hat in his hand and sticks his finger through a hole in the crown.)

Vir.—Mr. Snoggs (sniffling), don't talk so. (She walks toward him holding her handkerchief to her eyes.)

Jean.—Aunt is going to make love to him. I'll bring Harry, and we will peep through the door. Here's fun. (Exit.)

Vir.—Mr. Snoggs, since the day you saved me from a watery grave——

Snoggs—What watery grave ?

Vir.—In Switzerland. Have you forgotten ?

Snoggs (trying to suppress a laugh)—No ; I'll never forget that. Donkey—bray—kick—whizz—splash—scream—ha, ha. (Aside.) She thinks I saved her life. The water wasn't deep enough to drown a bag of puppies.

Vir.—I knew you would not forget it. You rescued me (sighs), my preserver.

Snoggs (aside)—She wasn't fairly ducked. (To Vir.) Yes, I fished you out. (Aside.) I think she is trying to fish me in. (To Vir.) Vicious mule.

Vir.—Yes ; Kabo was vicious.

Snoggs—Kabo ! (Aside.) Ayres calls me Kabo. He tells me it is because I have so much elasticity and tenacity, but I see he has named me after a donkey. Alas, how my friends despise me now ! (Sighs.)

Vir.—Why do you sigh ?

Snoggs—How can I tell you ?

Vir.—There is no need of telling me. I can read it in your eyes (ecstatically). Oh, Blackburne ! (Throws herself into his arms.)

Snoggs (aside)—Deuce take it, here's a scrape. I wonder if there's a hole to get out. (He edges toward the door, but hears a suppressed laugh and retreats from it.)

Vir.—Oh, Blackburne, I am so happy. (Remains in Snoggs' unwilling embrace, when the door opens and Jeannette and Ayres enter.)

Ayres—Aha, Kabo, I've caught you.

Snoggs—Don't call me Kabo. (Aside.) What a pickle I'm in.

Ayres—Kabo is all right. It's good corset material. (Points to Snoggs' arms around Virginia's waist.

Jean.—Of *cors-et* is.

Snoggs looses himself from Virginia and bolts from the room, leaving his hat on the floor. Virginia follows.

Enter JOHN SPOFFORD.

Spof.—What's the row ?

Ayres—Snoggs has been proposing to Miss Virginia.

Spof.—The old fool.

Jean.—I think it must have been Aunt Virginia that proposed to him.

Spof.—The old fooless.

Jean.—Papa, do not be so hard on them. Perhaps they love each other.

Spof.—Love nothing. Bah ! They make me sick. I think I'll go out and have something.

Ayres (detaining him)—But, Mr. Spofford, you should not lose sight of the advantages of such a union. Virginia would get what she has been longing for many years—a husband ; and Snoggs what he most needs—money.

Spof.—Virginia has just one thousand dollars in her fortune. Do you call that money ? Fiddlesticks !

Ayres—It is all that Snoggs needs. He has ability, and I would be willing to back him against any lawyer in the town if he only had a suit of clothes and a month's victuals. He has been unfortunate, but with a thousand dollars he will rise again,

Spof.—Come out and take something with me. (Exit with Ayres, followed by Jeannette.)

Enter SNOGGS. Endeavors to seize his hat and escape, but encounters Jeannette at the door.

Jeannette—Mr. Snoggs, do not be offended at Harry. Of course, he is fond of fun, but he means well by you. He is urging papa at this moment to give his consent to your marriage with Virginia.

Snoggs—Lord preserve me—but I don't want to marry Virginia.

Jeannette—Yes you do. I saw you have your arms around her. But perhaps it is only her fortune you crave.

Snoggs—Her fortune ?

Jeannette—Yes, her fortune. She has a thousand dollars.

Snoggs—A thousand dollars (with a gulp).

Exit Jeannette. Snoggs stands meditating. Enter Virginia. When she sees Snoggs she turns her back to him. Snoggs sidles up to her.

Snoggs—Virginia.
           (Virginia shrugs her shoulders.)

Snoggs—I say, Virginia. (Pokes her with his finger, but receives no answer). Virgy, my darling.

Vir.—Well, what is it ?

Snoggs—Come to my arms !

Vir.—Oh, Blackburne. (They embrace.)

Enter JEANNETTE, AYRES and SPOFFORD, the latter slightly tipsy, carrying a bottle.

Ayres—Whoa, Kabo !

Spof.—I say, Znoggz, take zomething with me.

Snoggs—Thanks, brother, for brother you will soon be. Allow me to present my bride.

Spof.—Thatz juzt what I've come in to talk about. You zee Harry here and myzelf have been talking it ovor. And Harry zayz, zayz he, here's Znoggz, zayz he (takes drink out of bottle)—Znoggz— zayz you—come and take something.

Ayres—Old man, you are getting pretty full. I think it is time to draw the curtain.

                CURTAIN.

A DISPUTE ABOUT CORSETS.

CHARACTERS.

Mrs. Winter, a lady of decided opinions.
Fanny Winter, her daughter.
Dr. Swartzbrod, a German physician.
Geoffrey Bantam, a dry-goods clerk, Fanny's betrothed.
Betsy Ann, the housemaid.

NOTE.—The broken English of the doctor and the dudish lisp of Bantam should be supplied by the persons acting the parts.

SCENE :—Mrs. Winter's Parlor.

As the curtain rises Mrs. Winter is discovered unwrapping a package containing two long boxes. She makes a gesture of impatience.

Mrs. Winter.—Well, I declare, this is aggravating. Now that young Bantam, on some occasions, shows rare good sense, but he is like all the rest of them, and flies off the handle if you don't hold him. When I expressly order Pinch's Corset he sends me a new fangled one that I have never tried. It is too provoking for anything ! I shall send them back. Oh, Geoffrey Bantam, I'll let you know whose daughter you are going to marry. There are many things I intend to teach you when you and Fanny are married, and I might as well begin now.

ENTER FANNY WINTER.

Fanny.—Why ma, you look angry—what has happened?
Mrs. W.—Why it's that young Bantam. If he'd stick a few feathers in his head no one would be able to tell the difference between him and his namesake in the back yard, who only opens his mouth to say kick-riki. I ordered Pinch's Corsets for us—and here is what he sent.
Fanny.—(Reads label)—Ball's Health Preserving Corset.—But mamma, judging from the advertisements these appear to be good. We had better try them.
Mrs. W.——Advertisements——fudge. But what ails you? You look tired.
Fanny.—I am suffering from a lame back, and my sides ache. I felt so unwell that I sent for Dr. Swartzbrod.

ENTER BETSY ANN.

B. A.—(Announcing) Dr. Swartzbrod. (Exit).

ENTER DR. SWARTZBROD.

Dr. S.—*Gutentag* Madame, it pleases me much you so well to see. Miss Fanny has for me sent. You not so well, Miss Fanny ?

Fanny.—No, doctor.

ENTER BETSY ANN.

B. A.—(Announcing) Mr. Bantam. (Aside) Come to see Miss Fanny, (exit).

ENTER GEOFFREY BANTAM.

Fanny.—Oh, Jeff ! I am so glad to see you.

Geoff.—My dear Fanny.

Mrs. W.—That will do. Save some of that hugging until a year after you are married. It will be scarcer then and more appreciated.

Dr. S.—Ach, my dear Madame, a year after they married are is love-making one humbug !

(Fanny goes to the doctor and engages him in conversation, while Mrs. W. beckons Bantam and points menacingly at the table. B. approaches tremblingly.)

Ban.—Wh—what is it ?

Mrs. W.—Didn't I say I wanted Pinch's Corset ?

Bant.—Y—yes, ma'am. But—

Mrs. W.—But what?

Bant.—But you said they were uncomfortable, and had defects, and so—and so—

Dr. S.—When I in the university was, and hunger had, drew I a sausage on a slate. Then fetched I myself a pint beer and slice bread. Then wiped I a piece sausage away, ate a piece bread and drank a swallow beer. Then drank I another swallow beer, ate another piece bread and wiped another piece sausage away. When I through was, I pictured myself in that I a sausage ate to my slice bread and pint beer. So it is with you. You get one new corset and wear it one time; you feel compressed everywhere. You wear it one time again and it feels not so bad. You wear it until it what you call broken in is. Then you say it fit. But it fits no more as I ate sausage. The corset has not adjusted itself to your shape, but your shape itself has adjusted to the corset. If you always sometimes would not wear it, your health would be better.

Fanny—But, Doctor, it is impossible not to wear a corset at all times. Cannot health be maintained without sacrificing the corset.

Geof. B.—Why yes, Fanny; as I was about to remark to your m—

Dr. S.—(Interrupting) There is one corset—only one—no more—that does not in the same way act. My notice to it was called by testimonials from doctors who are all over known.

Bant.—Yes, Doctor, as I was about to remark to Mrs. W——

Dr. S.—(interrupting)—This corset the first time fits. It no breaking in needs, and it to the movements of the body yields.

Fanny—And that corset is?

Bant.—I am sure it can be no other than——

Dr. S.—(Interrupting)—That is called Ball's Health Preserving Corset.

Bant.—Now, Mrs. W——

Dr. S.—(Interrupting)—Ah, I see you have already some bought It is like the proverb, speak of corsets and you hear the snapping of the whalebones.

Bant.—But, Doctor——

Dr. S.—(Interrupting)—Only, you know, these no whale-bones have. They Kabo-boned are. Kabo don't snap.

Enter Betsy Ann.

Bant.—Just so, Doctor, and I may add——

Dr. S.—(Interrupting again, and eyeing him savagely. While the Doctor is talking, Bantam retreats under his glance, until he runs into Betsy Ann, who handles him roughly)—Now Mr. Bantam, if you will let me say one single word—only one word. You have had your say, let me a word in get. (To Mrs. W.) I want to on you urge always to wear these corsets—both you and Miss Fanny, and you both as healthy will be as *that* (pointing to Betsy Ann).

Bant.—Yes, as healthy as *that* (pointing to Betsy Ann).

B. A.—(Goes up to Bantam) As what (shakes her fist under his nose. He retires behind Fanny.)

Dr. S.—Ha, ha. Fraulein, what corset you wear.

(B. A. bashfully puts her hands to her face and titters.)

Fanny—Do not blush for Jeff's sake.

B. A.—No, indeed, I'm not blushing for his sake—its for my own sake.—If he calls me *that* again, I'll fix him so *he'll* have to wear corsets. (Then in a very loud whisper to Mrs. W.) I wear Ball's Corsets.

Mrs. W.—Jeff, I was going to rate you severely, but I'll postpone it for a while. The next opportunity I have I shall make up for letting you off so easily this time.

B. A.—(Aside) You bet.   (Aloud) Me too.

(Curtain.)

CHARADES.

Among the most enjoyable of parlor entertainments are charades. They offer splendid opportunity for the exercise of the wits and are apt to create fun for all concerned. They may be acted either as panto-mines or as short dialogues. If words are used, care should be taken to use the word intended to be guessed as little as possible and only in such connections where it will not be noticed particularly.

We give below some words which may be used for acting char-ades, together with some hints for their proper presentation:

PETTICOAT.—*Pet*—May be represented by bringing a small child upon the stage, very much caressed and very much spoiled. Or, if a par-rot or other animal is handy, it can be brought in to good advantage.

Tie—A lady tying a gentleman's necktie or making a great fuss about tying up a bundle, will convey this syllable.

Coat—A gentleman who has a very dilapidated coat trying to get it mended, or a conversation about a coat of paint.

The full word may be illustrated by a lady in costume, or, if words are used, by an angry dispute between a supposed husband and wife, opened by his declaring that he does not propose to submit to petticoat rule.

BRIDEWELL.—*Bride*—A mock marriage ceremony in which the bride is of course the central figure, or a dialogue between a newly mar-ried couple in which the bride shows her teeth and worsts her better half.

Well—A representation of the Biblical legend of Rebecca at the well, or a farcical talk about a well.

The whole word can be illustrated by bringing in a prisoner in chains and assigning him his place on a bench and giving him a shoe on which he must go to work as if soling it.

DYNAMITE—*Die*—A death-bed scene, or conversation relating to death—do not make this too somber, as it may awake memories in the breasts of some.

Nay—A comic love scene in which the lady refuses the hand of a gentleman.

Mite—A beggar receiving alms, or a bit of some article good to eat given to some one apparently very hungry.

The whole word.—Bring in a foot-ball with a piece of lamp-wick in the vent hole and make a great ado about lighting and bursting it.

DUMB-WAITER.—This can be represented only with dialogue.

Dumb—A stupid boy who is being taught something and is not able to comprehend what is said.

Waiter—A tray can be brought in incidentally in a conversation.

The whole word may be laughably illustrated by a foolish waiter who makes all sorts of mistakes.

PANTOMIMES.

When pantomimes are in order everybody is prepared to laugh, and it is important to have everything of as huge and grotesque a pattern as it is possible to make it. Such things as scissors, razors, knives, saws, and other articles of that description must be monstrosities and can be made of straw or card-board, painted gray, to resemble steel. There are other things which should be made exceedingly small, such as drums, trumpets, hand carts and other articles used by small boys in play. The rule generally is to go to the other extreme—making small articles large and large articles small. Articles of wear that fit are out of place in a pantomime; a hat must be either ridiculously small or large; the same may be said of parasols, overcoats and shoes. It is not necessary to give other general instructions than these, because pantomimes are all the more laughable if ridiculous blunders are made.

We give a few which may be acted with great effect:

THE NEW BOY.

The scene discloses what purports to be a doctor's office. The doctor sits in his dressing-gown and paints a sign, "Boy Wanted," on a card and goes outside the door with it. Immediately after he returns a woman and an over-grown boy appear. The boy's pantaloons are not nearly long enough and his sleeves pinch him very much. He is sucking a large stick of candy. The doctor does not appear to like the boy, but the woman gesticulates violently, shakes first her finger and then her fists at the doctor, who finally appears cowed and accepts the boy.

The woman goes out. The doctor hands the boy a feather duster, intimating that he should dust the articles in the room, and takes up a book. He looks up and finds the boy still sucking his candy. Takes candy away, throws it into cuspidore, and makes the boy start dusting. Then he resumes his reading. As soon as his back is turned the boy picks candy from cuspidore and begins eating again. Doctor looks up, siezes candy and throws it out of doors. Boy cries. Doctor cuffs his ears and makes him go to work. He resumes his reading. Boy brushes some things, including book in doctor's hands, doctor's face and the back of his head. When he dusts a cupboard or shelf he takes a bottle with a large " poison " label upon it, examines it gleefully, takes out cork and sips a little. He is immediately convulsed, and cries " Ow! ow! ow!" Woman rushes in, doctor sees label on bottle and rushes out. Returns with an umbrella. Woman takes a knife from a box on the table and viciously approaches the doctor. Boy falls to the floor. Doctor points to the bottle and the woman tears her hair in dismay. Doctor goes to the boy and sticks end of umbrella in his mouth and opens and shuts it several times rapidly, in imitation of a stomach pump. Boy rises. They all join in a three-handed embrace. Curtain.

WOOING UNDER DIFFICULTIES.

The scene represents an old lady in a corner sound asleep. In the foreground are a young lady and gentleman evidently very spoony, but whenever the youth tries to put his arm around the maiden's waist the old lady snorts and opens her eyes. An idea seems to strike the youth. He goes out and returns immediately with a bundle of clothes. He stands one chair upon another immediately before the old lady and covers them with clothes so as to completely obstruct her view. As he is about to resume his former place a small boy comes in, whose face lights up with joy when he sees the backs of the two lovers. He takes from his pocket a paper ball tied to a string, and, hiding behind the covered chairs, he pesters the ardent swain with the ball, until the latter jumps up furiously and rushes behind the chairs. The boy, however, runs around them and manages to escape being seen. He then resumes his seat beside the bashful girl, who has not dared to look up during all this time, but he continually looks up furtively, evidently expecting another attack. The boy peeps out, throws his ball, but is discovered by the youth. Boy runs, but is followed closely. Boy steps upon the old lady's toe, who jumps up and violently boxes the ears of the young man, who, coming after the boy, got there just in time to receive her cuffs. The young man assumes a highly indignant air, stalks out of the room, returns with his hat in hand, and, with a stately bow, retires. The maiden begins to cry and gesticulates violently before her mother, intimating that she had driven him away. Old lady looks horror-stricken for a few moments, but, seeing the boy, she pounces upon him, and both of the ladies chastise him severely. The boy bawls loudly, and the curtain drops upon the pathetic scene.

A RESTAURANT SCENE.

Several tables are spread and people may be eating at them or not, whichever is convenient. A pompous-looking man comes in and sits down at one of the tables. A shuffling waiter, who is constantly stumbling against things and dropping his tray, sidles up to him and puts his ear near the man's mouth. He evidently gets the order and disappears. The man takes up a bottle from the table, uncorks it, and smells its contents. He is seized with a violent fit of sneezing. Waiter comes in with tray and plates, running against the sneezing head, drops his tray and dishes, and rushes out again in time to escape a vigorous kick aimed at him by the man, who shakes his fist after him, and then picks up the dishes. The waiter reappears with a bowl of soup, and, timidly approaching, gets it down on the table safely and escapes. The man is about to eat when he suddenly throws down his spoon and beckons viciously for the waiter. The latter approaches very much scared. The man pulls a long hair out of the soup. (The hair should be thread, so that the audience can see it.) The waiter appears dismayed, rushes out and returns with the cook, who has her sleeves rolled up and carries a soup ladle. When she sees the hair, she shakes her head, denying that it was hers. A lady, evidently the proprietress, comes up and appears to insist that it is the cook's hair. The man, proprietress and cook begin gesticulating violently and pounding with their fists upon the table. The waiter attempts to put in an oar, but is silenced by the cook, who hits him in the eye with the ladle. When the row is at its height, a girl with her sleeves rolled up appears, dressed like a second girl in a kitchen, and, taking the hair, compares it with her own, to the satisfaction of all, especially the man who discovered it, who smiles and throws kisses at her as the curtain goes down.

A TRIBUTE TO THE LADIES.

What is more beautiful to look upon than a finely-formed, well dressed and graceful woman. She flits before you, a model of grace and beauty, and when she is gone you feel as if you were better for having been in her presence.

You grumblers that cannot find beauty in anything, just visit the Fashion skating rink and watch the beautiful creatures (the ladies, I mean) as they glide over the polished floor. It seems as if they were floating through space on fairy wings; their every move is grace; and after looking upon this scene, if you do not say there is grace and beauty combined, you ought to be deprived of ever associating with the fair creatures.

It is the duty of every lady to appear to the best advantage possible, and in order to do this she must be well dressed. No dress can fit perfectly unless she wear a corset. It has been a problem for a long time what corset to buy that will add grace and beauty to the form without injury to the wearer. The Chicago Corset Co. have overcome this difficulty by inventing their Ball's Coiled Wire Spring Elastic Section Corset.—*Herald.*

A POOR WIFE.

A tourist on the Mississippi listened to the complaints of a mountaineer about hard times for ten or fifteen minutes, and then said :

"Why, man, you ought to get rich shipping green corn to the northern market."

"Yes, I orter," was the reply.

"You have the land, I suppose, and can get the seed?"

"Yes."

"Then why don't you go into the speculation?"

"No use, stranger," replied the native; "my wife's too lazy to do the plowin' and plantin'."

A well-known brother of the press remarks in a recent issue: "It is not our fault that we are red-headed and small, and the next time one of those overgrown rural roosters in a ball-room reaches down for my head, and suggests that some one has lost a rose-bud out of his button-hole, there will be trouble."

H. P. ABDOMINAL.

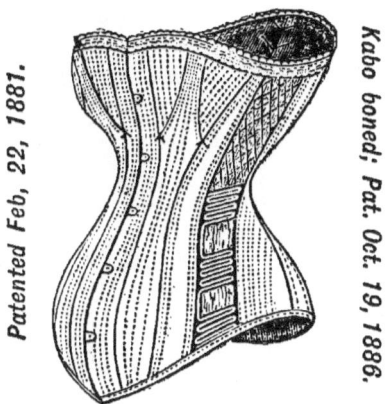

Patented Feb, 22, 1881.

Kabo boned; Pat. Oct. 19, 1886.

This Corset is made extra long, fourteen and a half inch heavy front steels being used, and heavy material throughout. In the larger sizes it is especially adapted to stout ladies who desire a long front, substantial Corset, and in the smaller sizes, to those who wish a long Corset. The elastic section extends from the bottom about half way to the top, as shown in the cut, and affords an easy and comfortable abdominal support. The abdominal fullness in this Corset is graded according to the size of the Corset, which adapts it successfully to the wants of both stout and tall, slender ladies who wish a long Corset. It need only to be worn to be appreciated.

Made from extra heavy satteen jean, sizes 19 to 36.

NEW HAVEN, CONN., Nov. 2, 1881.

I have examined BALL'S HEALTH CORSET, and have no hesitation in saying that it is in my opinion, the best I have ever seen. I can not see how, with one of these corsets, it will be possible to practice tight lacing. If you can succeed in bringing it into general use, you will confer a great blessing on the females of our country.

Very truly yours,   P. A. JEWETT, M.D.

H. P. EXTRA LONG.

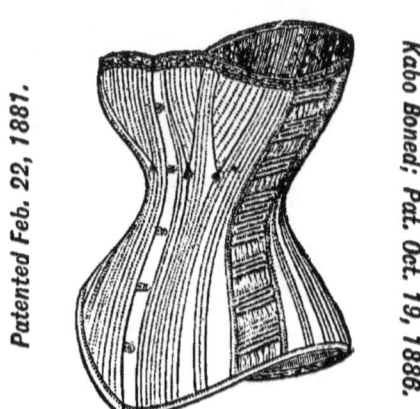

Patented Feb. 22, 1881.

Kabo Boned; Pat. Oct. 19, 1886.

Ball's Extra Long Corset is similar in construction to our Health Preserving, but is considerably longer and has five hook steels. It will meet the wants of those who prefer a long-waisted Corset.

Made in white and drab satteen jean, in sizes from 18 to 36.

Testimony of Madame SCALCHI, the World-Renowned Contralto.

THE GRAND PACIFIC HOTEL, JOHN B. DRAKE & Co., Proprietors, CHICAGO, April 18th, 1885.—*Dear Sir:* The Ball Corset you had the kindness to send me deserves so high praise that I wish be able to express myself in your language better than I can do. Please accept my thanks for it, and believe me,   Yours truly,

SOFIE SCALCHI LOLLY.

PARLOR MAGIC.

In this department the aim will be, not so much to explain or teach the marvelous sleight of hand performances that we wonder at when we see them done by skilful conjurers, but rather to illustrate some innocent deception which can be performed without expense, at any gathering, and with the aid of only such materials as are always found in a household. For instance, every house contains at least one pack of cards; and the numberless tricks which may be performed with this pack of cards will be found a source of endless amusement. We append a few, which, with a little ingenuity on the part of the performer, may be varied so as to appear new each time they are attempted :

TO DISCOVER A CARD DRAWN.

Turn upside down the card at the bottom of the pack. Then request that a card be drawn, and after it is drawn, unobserved by anyone turn the pack upside down. When the card is replaced you turn your back to the audience, run through the pack, and the one turned wrong is the drawn card.

Another way of performing this trick is to cut off a very small portion of one end of a pack of cards, just enough to make a difference in the margin discernable. Then having the small margins all turned one way, you shuffle the pack and allow one to be drawn. Quickly reverse the pack in your hands; when the card is replaced, the small margin is not on the same side with the others and you can easily single it out.

TO DISCOVER A CARD THOUGHT OF.

Take twenty-one cards, spread them out, and ask some one to think of one of the cards and remember where you place it. Gathering up the cards you begin laying them out in three piles, one card at a time. When they are all laid out ask in which pile the card thought of is. When told gather up the three piles, with the pile containing that card between the other two. Do this three times. Then count from either end of the pack up to the eleventh card, which will be the one you are seeking.

SLEIGHT-OF-HAND TRICKS WITH CARDS.

Persons who wish to become skilful in the manipulation of cards must practice a great deal and learn to be quick in their movements, although sleight-of-hand consists more in diverting the attention of an audience than the quick movements. After some practice they will find the accomplishments of "palming" a card, "making a pass," forcing" a card, making a false shuffle, and "sighting" a card, of great service.

To palm a card: Take the card up in the palm of the hand by slightly bending it, and inserting one corner immediately below the ball of the thumb, while the corner diagonally opposite from it should be held between the third and little finger. The bend of the hand should be a natural one, so that the audience does not notice that you are concealing something in it.

To force a card: In asking persons to select a card from a pack it is often desirable that they should take one which you must force upon them. Push the one you wish to force a little beyond the rest when holding out the pack spread out. Most people will take the handiest card and you will have no difficulty. Sometimes the person drawing does not reach for the one you have pushed out. It is then that your skill in forcing is brought to a test. You must divert his attention while he is drawing, and, in place of the one he thinks he is taking, you must push the forced card into his hand; or you can quickly transpose the position of the cards, when he is apt to refuse the one he had reached for and take the card you wish him to take. If the person drawing is very persistent, however, in refusing the forced card, throw up the pack on some pretext and pass him by. Forcing is difficult sometimes even for experts.

To make a pass: It is very easy to get a glimpse of the card at the bottom of the pack; therefore, to be able to remove it and place it in another part of the pack unobserved often makes a difficult trick an easy one.

To make a false shuffle: This is done best by actually shuffling a small portion of the pack, always taking care that the part which is not to be shuffled is held firm between the fingers.

To sight a card: Your ability to sight a card will, of course, depend somewhat upon the watchfulness of the others. If you have a chance to take the card in the hand you can almost always, by a quick movement, tilt it so that the face is visible for an instant.

A SIMPLE TRICK.

The court cards almost invariably have a little more margin on one side than the other. Lay out four cards with the large margins all turned the same way, and then ask some one to turn around one of the cards while you are out, announcing that you can go out of the room and yet be able to show which card has been turned around. When you come back if the large margin on one of the cards is not on the same side as the others you know it has been turned around. If you repeat the trick do not turn around this card, as that will perhaps be noticed, but carefully observe the position the cards are in, and detect the turned one as before. Though simple, this trick is very perplexing to the uninitiated.

TO CALL OFF THE CARDS IN A PACK WHICH IS TURNED UPSIDE DOWN.

Take a sentence of thirteen words and learn to associate each word with a card of a certain value. One like the following is easily learned:

Seven regiments battled with nine, when the king and eight thousand men arrived.
  7   10   3   6   9   5   2   king queen 8   ace   knave   4

Spreading out the pack you pick up the cards in this order, alternating the different suits. When you have gathered the pack it can be cut an indefinite number of times, yet you will have the clew to the whole by simply taking up the top card. You can read off one after another through the entire deck without looking at another card, causing the utmost surprise to the uninitiated.

TO CAUSE A CARD DRAWN TO RISE OUT OF THE PACK.

Take two cards and cut a notch at one end of each. Fasten the ends of a small broken rubber band in the notches, leaving enough between the cards to admit of being stretched the full length of the cards. Offer the pack to any one, and bid him draw a card and look at it. When he replaces the card you must have the pack opened in such a way that he will put it between the cards connected by the band. Force the card down and hold firmly so that no one will notice that it would pop up if not. held that way. Then ask what card was drawn. The drawer says, for instance, "The ace of hearts." You then say, "Ace of hearts arise and show yourself," at the same time slightly loosen your pressure on the pack, and the ace of hearts will gracefully ascend until more than half of the card is above the pack.

THE BOOMERANG.

Cut out of card a miniature boomerang about this size and shape:

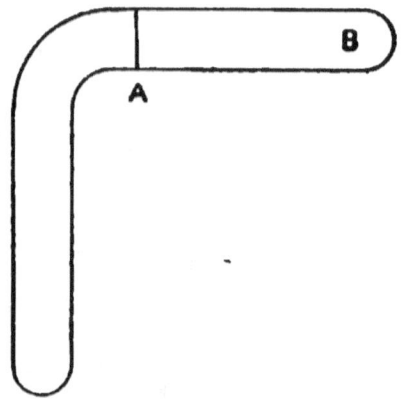

Rest it upon a book or other article which can be held in the hand, leaving everything to the right of a project from the.edge. Taking up the book, by giving the end b a sharp tap, the boomerang can be made to fly a long distance, when it will rise in the air and return, falling almost at the feet of the person who has sent it.

TO RESTORE A RIBBON AFTER IT IS DESTROYED.

Secure two pieces of ribbon of exactly the same size and color. Moisten one side of one of them and press against the palm of the hand. It will stick there and can easily be concealed by bending the hand a little. Then take the other and allow it to be torn into shreds and burned upon a plate. After the ribbon has been destroyed you take up the ashes and immerse in a bowl of water which has been examined by the audience. Then putting in your hand you draw forth the concealed ribbon, apparently restored by the action of the water.

A LOVE TEST.

Put some powdered quick lime into a wine bottle nearly full of water and shake occasionally for a day or two. Then pour off the water from the sediment. This apparently pure water is as clear as any you would draw from a spring; but if blown into it becomes white as milk. Having your lime water in readiness you can announce to an audience that you have discovered a means of finding out which of the young ladies present are in love and which of them are not; that you will provide each with a glass of water and a straw; if the water turns into milk upon being blown into, it is a sign that the blower has lost her heart, while if it remains clear she is still free to choose. A clever guess will enable you to hand out the lime water to parties whose blushes will subsequently establish the truth of the test, while to others you hand tumblers of pure water. This little trick can be played with startling effect.

TO EXTRACT A CORK. FROM A BOTTLE WITHOUT TOUCHING THE CORK.

Fill a bottle full of water or other liquid, and cork it so tightly that the bottom of the cork is flushed with the liquid. Wrap the bottle round the bottom with a thick cloth, and knock it against some immovable object. The motion of the liquid acting as a solid body should force out the cork.

CLAIRVOYANCE.

To puzzle an audience with what appears to be the power of "second sight" or clairvoyance, requires some skill, an accurate memory, and more or less practice.

The favorite mode of procedure is to securely blindfold the person alleged to be possessed of this wonderful power, when a confederate goes among the audience taking articles from them at random and asking the blindfolded person to describe them.

This is done by means of what may be termed a cipher code adopted and studied beforehand. A few illustrations will suffice to make it clear. By studying the questions and answers given below it will be seen that the word printed in italics gives the cue to the distinctive properties of the article while the general wording of the question informs the blindfolded person what the article is:

What do I *hold* in my hand ? A silver watch.

What do I *carry* in my hand ? A gold watch.

What do I *hold* in my hand now ? A silver watch and chain.

What do I *carry* in my hand how ? A gold watch and chain.

What do I *carry* now ? A gold locket and chain.

Do you see what I *carry* in my hand ? Yes, it is a gold ring.

What have I just taken *up* ? A silk hat.

What is *this* I have in my hand ? A small pen knife.

What have I in my hand ? A glove.

Of course the more experienced ones have a more elaborate code than the one illustrated above, but the principle is the same. Sometimes an article is given the person asking the questions which has not been thought of in preparing the code. In those cases it is best for him to devise some means of returning the object without questioning the blindfolded person, but if pressed to do so he can find some way of communicating with his confederate by means of a preconcerted rule. One of the favorite methods is to word the question so that the first letter of each word will spell the name of the object. For instance if a *bottle* is handed the questioner, he might say. "That is a suspicious looking article to have about you, *but only to take little evenings* will do no harm. What is it ?" He must slightly accent the words containing the cue, and be careful not to make a mistake.

HOW TO FIND THE NUMBER OF POINTS IN EACH DIE THROWN.

Tell the person who cast the dice to double the number of points upon one of them, and add 5 to it; then to multiply the sum produced by 5, and to add to the product the number of points upon the other die. This being done, desire him to tell you the amount, and having thrown out 25, the remainder will be a number consisting of two figures, the first of which, to the left, is the number of points on the first die, and the second figure, to the right, the number of the other. Thus :

Suppose the number of points of the first die which comes up to be 2, and that of the other 3; then, if to 4, the double of the points of the first, there be added 5, and the sum produced, 9, be multiplied by 5, the product will be 45; to which, if 3, the number of points on the other die, be added, 48 will be produced, from which, if 25 be subtracted, 23 will remain, the first figure of which is 2, the number of points on the first die, and the second figure, 3, the number on the other.

TO EXTRACT EGGS FROM AN EMPTY BAG.

This trick consists in making what appears to be a bag of coarse cloth, lined, but is in reality two bags, one inside of the other, sewed together at the top. At the bottom of the inner bag, pockets should be made which can be reached through slits in the cloth. Fill these pockets with eggs (hollow ones are best). You turn the bag inside out several times to convince everyone that there is nothing in the bag. Then announce that you will manufacture an egg by simply blowing into the bag. Blow in and take out an egg from one of the pockets, to the amazement of the audience. Much fun can be had out of some one in the audience, by providing yourself with a very small egg in one of the pockets. You ask the person selected to try his hand at blowing, and see if he can make an egg. After he has blown, you look into the bag and declare that he hasn't blown hard enough, and ask him to blow again. He will blow harder. Still insist that he must blow harder. When he has fairly blown his lungs out and the audience is convulsed with laughter at his antics, insert your hand in the bag and draw out the small egg, and congratulate him on his first attempt at manufacturing eggs, assuring him that in the course of time he will be able to produce a size more apt to command a ready sale.

BURNING ICE.

An audience can often be astonished by what appears to be burning ice or water. By making a hole in a cake of ice and pouring in some spirits of camphor, the latter can be set fire to, and the impression created that the ice itself is burning.

Sodium and potassium are chemicals which will burn very brightly when they touch water or ice, but we would not recommend their use by any but experts, on account of their disposition to splutter, which might result in the loss of an eyesight, if handled by a person who is not accustomed to them.

A small taper can be burned for a few seconds under water in the following manner: Set it afloat on the water and light it. Then inverting a tumbler directly over it, you quickly plunge it beneath the water. The air in the tumbler will prevent the water from filling it and the taper can, for a few moments, be seen burning brightly, apparently surrounded by water.

HOW TO CONVERT PAPER SHAVINGS INTO RIBBONS.

Quite a large amount of ribbon can be concealed in the mouth at a time by rolling up tightly. Have a roll as large as you can hide in readiness, and proceed to tell the audience that you have discarded the ordinary food which other people eat—that you have found something far more wholesome. Then bring in a lot of paper shavings. A bookbinder can give you a few handfuls, which, when shaken up well, appear to be an enormous pile. You begin to chew at them, taking every opportunity you can to withdraw what you have in your mouth and dropping them on the floor. The table at which you sit should have a cloth reaching down to the ground, so that everything back of it is concealed. By this means you will be able, occasionally, under pretense of taking a very large mouthful, to push a bunch of the shavings down.

When you are nearing the end you declare that you have eaten a hearty meal, but that it does not seem to be agreeing with you; that they should not be alarmed if they were to witness a startling phenomenon, as your digestive apparatus is subject to all sorts of freaks. Then slip the ribbon into your mouth, and make a very wry face. Catching one end of the ribbon, you begin to pull at it slowly. After you have drawn out several yards of it cease drawing, but pretend you are still doing so. The effect is the same as if you were continually drawing out more ribbon. When the fun has been long enough prolonged, finish by drawing out the balance of the ribbon and declare that you feel better now.

TO PUT WATER INTO A TUMBLER WHEN UPSIDE DOWN.

Take a plate containing some water and place upon it an empty tumbler. Then burn some brandy or spirits of wine in the glass, and as the flame is disappearing quickly invert the glass. The water will rush into the glass with great violence.

GUESSING THE TWO ENDS OF A LINE OF DOMINOES.

You can go out of a room in which a game of dominoes is in progress, saying that when they finish their game you can come back and tell them what two numbers are at the extremes of the lines without looking at them. The trick consists in securing, unobserved, one of the dominoes (not a double). Whatever it is, if the balance are laid down according to the rules of the game, the two ends of the line have the same number on them as on the missing dominoe.

TOLD HIM.

It takes moral courage to say " I don't know," and whether the following anecdote is true or not, it illustrates a phase of character that is not uncommon:

" Father," said a young Hibernian, " what's a gondola?"

" A gondola, is it?"

" Yes."

" It's a koind of vegetable that grows in Italy. Yis, and it tastes something loike a puttater."

" Yis, sor. And what's a sultan?"

" A sooltan, is it?"

" Yes."

" A sooltan is a musical instrument that performs loike a hand-orgin."

" Yis, sor. Thank ye, sor! An' what's a giraffe?"

" A giraffe, did ye say?"

" Yes, a giraffe."

" A giraffe? Wall, now, Jimmy, it's a good while since I studied aljabry, but ef I remimber, it's one of them things that the haythen set down on when they drink their tay."

" It must take a lot of experience to learn so much."

" Ay, ay, my son, that i, does."

WEDDING ANNIVERSARIES.

First	Anniversary	Paper
Fifth	"	Wooden.
Tenth	"	Tin.
Fifteenth	"	Crystal.
Twentieth	"	China.
Twenty-fifth	"	Silver.
Thirtieth	"	Cotton.
Thirty-fifth	"	Linen.
Fortieth	"	Woolen.
Forty-fifth	"	Silk.
Fiftieth	"	Golden.
Seventy-fifth	"	Diamond.

HANDKERCHIEF FLIRTATIONS.

Drawing across the lips—Desiring a flirtation.
Twisting in the left hand—I wish to be rid of you.
Winding it around the third finger—I am married.
Winding it around the fore finger—I am engaged.
Putting it in the pocket—No more love at present.
Letting it remain on the eyes—You are so cruel.
Opposite corners in both hands—Do wait for me.
Twisting it in the right hand—I love another.
Drawing it through the hands—I hate you.
Letting it rest on the right cheek—Yes.
Letting it rest on the left cheek—No.
Twirling in both hands—Indifference.
Drawing across the eyes—I am sorry.
Drawing across the cheek—I love you.
Folding it—I wish to speak with you.
Dropping—We will be friends.
Over the shoulder—Follow me.

—A balky horse and a man "who knows it all" are the best means of teaching us the value of patience.—*Fall River Advance.*

—Some women never fully value a husband until he has been killed in an accident, and they see a chance to recover damages.

WHAT EMINENT PHYSICIANS SAY OF BALL'S CORSETS.

NEW HAVEN, CONN., July 6, 1882.

I have examined the BALL HEALTH-PRESERVING CORSET, and have had for some time several patients wearing them. From my investigation I am thoroughly satisfied that it has merits above any other Corset made. W. G. ALLING, M.D.

NEW HAVEN, CONN., Dec. 5, 1881.

In my opinion, BALL'S HEALTH-PRESERVING CORSET is a thorough success, and does all you claim for it. In cases where physicians, as a rule, would recommend that corsets be discarded altogether, it is capable of affording great comfort, because it will support the body without causing compression. F. L. DIBBLE, M.D.

CHICAGO, October 23, 1880.

I have examined BALL'S HEALTH-PRESERVING CORSET, and believe that it is in every respect best calculated to preserve the health of the woman who wears it. It does not seem possible for the wearer of such a corset to be injured by tight lacing. It should receive the favorable endorsement of the physicians who have opportunity of examining it. JAMES NEVINS HYDE.

CHICAGO, October 26, 1880.

I fully endorse what Dr. Hyde says in the above note. W. H. BYFORD.

CHICAGO, October 13, 1880.

I have examined BALL'S HEALTH-PRESERVING CORSET, and believe it to be the least injurious to the wearer of any corset I have seen. A. J. BAXTER, M.D.

CHICAGO, October 27, 1880.

I do not advise any woman to wear a corset, but if she WILL do so—and she generally will—I advise her to use one of BALL'S HEALTH-PRESERVING CORSETS, as it is less likely to do her injury than any with which I am acquainted, A. REEVES JACKSON,

H. P. NURSING.

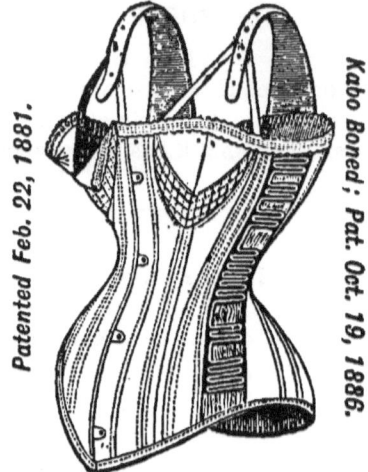

Patented Feb. 22, 1881.

Kabo Boned; Pat. Oct. 19, 1886.

In this Corset the cut of the lower part of the bust, being like a cup-shaped shelf standing at nearly a right angle with the body of the Corset, combined with the arrangement of the shoulder straps, affords entire relief to the muscles of the upper part of the breast of its wearer by sustaining the weight from the shoulder. This, together with the convenient arrangement of the upper part of the bust for exposing the whole breast to the child when desired, and the perfect ease and comfort afforded by the elastic section in the body of the Corset, renders this the *only* satisfactory Nursing Corset, and free from the many objections found in all others.

Made from satteen jean, white and drab. Sizes 18 to 30.

Testimony of Madame FURSCH-MADI, the Prima Donna.

THE GRAND PACIFIC HOTEL, JOHN B. DRAKE & Co., Proprietors, CHICAGO, April 18, 1885.—*Dear Sir:* After having tried "Ball's Corsets" I find them in quality superior to any I have used before. I heartily recommend them to the public.

E. FURSCH-MADI.

GUARANTEE.

Any lady purchasing one of Ball's Corsets may return it, after wearing it three weeks, to the dealer from whom it was bought, if not found

Perfectly * Satisfactory * in * Every * Respect,

and the price paid for it will be refunded by him; and if unsalable, the price paid by him will be refunded by us on its return to

CHICAGO CORSET CO.

BALL'S H. P. MISSES' CORSET.

FITS PERFECTLY

And yields readily to every breath and motion of its wearer. The only Misses' Corset approved by physicians as not injurious.

Patented Feb. 22, 1881. Kabo Boned; Pat. Oct. 19, 1886.

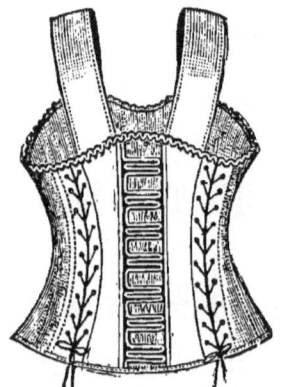

BACK VIEW.

Train your daughters to a healthy and symmetrical body and mind, and existence becomes a delight. Last in our Catalogue, but first in importance, because of its effects on our daughters, is our

H. P. MISSES' CORSET.

Every mother will recognize and appreciate the value of this Corset over all others for her daughter if she does not that of our other Corsets for herself. It fits closely and perfectly, and in its elasticity admits perfect freedom of movement, room for growth and full respiration. It is the *ne plus ultra* of Misses' Corsets.

Made from satteen jean, white and drab. Sizes 18 to 26.

TABLEAUX.

Tableaux may be classed among the more elaborate of parlor amusements, requiring preparation and accessories. They can be made very effective if some attention is given to detail.

Among the articles at hand should be an assortment of chalk of various colors, some gauze, and if stormy scenes or battle-scenes are depicted, an oblong piece of sheet iron about 3½ feet long and two feet wide.

Thunder may be imitated by hanging up the sheet-iron at one end and shaking the other end. The distant booming of artillery, by striking with a large drum stick. An alarm or fire-bell by striking at regular intervals with a metal rod.

Wrinkles can be made with black chalk; the hair whitened with chalk; poverty or sickness can be suggested by blue chalk marks under the eyes and in the hollows of the cheeks.

Parlors that are divided by sliding doors are easily arranged for tableaux. A curtain can, however, be easily improvised from almost any material. It is best to hang it on heavy wire, since nothing is of greater importance than a well managed curtain.

We give below a few striking scenes which may be represented.

They are merely illustrations of what can be done with very limited resources.

POCAHONTAS SAVING THE LIFE OF CAPTAIN SMITH.

Captain Smith lies upon the ground, with a block of wood where his head would be if it were not held in the left arm of Pocahontas, who is kneeling on one knee, and warding off the expected blow with the right hand. The executioner stands beside them with an uplifted club, while Powhattan stands a little behind this group in an attitude of suddenly arrested speech, while his face expresses surprise. There are

Indians kneeling, sitting and standing about, who all appear to be struck with apprehension.

Pocahontas' costume is a short cloth skirt trimmed with fringe and colored beads, a waist without sleeves trimmed in the same way, with flesh colored hose, mocassins and feathered head dress. Bracelets of brass or beads should be on her wrists and ankles. Her hair should be flowing.

Powhattan and the other Indians can be attired in overalls of various colors, with bright fringe trimmings and feather head-dress, belts around their waist, containing tomahawks, knives, scalps and so forth, and mocassins on their feet. Powhattan should be attired more showily than the rest and should wear a cloak.

John Smith should have a brown coat, a black belt, a large white collar or ruff, full gray breeches, brown hose, black shoes with buckles and a black felt hat with a broad red ribbon on it.

By burning red light on the stage, and turning the lights before the stage very low this can be made an impressive tableau.

THE VOLUNTEER—IN THREE TABLEAUX.

TABLEAU I.—OFF TO THE WAR.

This represents the soldier leaving home. He stands as if about to depart, reaching for a musket which his sister, who is weeping, hands to him, while his wife clings to him, as if trying to detain him. An aged woman, his mother, kneels in prayer, while his father is endeavoring to restrain a small boy, the soldier's son, who is decked out with toy military trappings and is brandishing a small sword, the spirit of patriotism evidently having possession of him, although too young to fight.

The volunteer should be attired in a military uniform, while the rest can dress in a manner becoming their parts without going to any expense.

TABLEAU II.—THE SOLDIER'S DREAM.

When the curtain rises the stage should be dark. The volunteer of the former tableau lies upon the ground asleep, beside a camp-fire. The latter can be arranged by piling several sticks of wood upon each other and inserting bits of gold paper here and there among them. After the soldier has been disclosed a curtain back of him is slowly raised, revealing a raised stage, brightly lit up, with the same characters as in the first tableau. A man with clothes exactly like the sleeping soldier's is seated in an arm-chair, holding the boy upon his knee. His wife is seated on the floor beside him, her head resting upon his lap. The old man and the sister are seated at a table on which is a lamp, she evidently reading aloud to the family, while the mother sits in the background nodding in sleep.

TABLEAU III.—THE RETURN.

Here the soldier appears in an officer's dress, with sword and epaulettes. The scene represents him as just arriving. A green cloth should be upon the floor of the stage in imitation of grass, the family meeting him before the house. The soldier is embracing his mother, the two being inclined in such a way as to give the impression that they had just flown into each others arms. The wife is running toward him with outstretched arms, while the sister and father appear dazed with joy and surprise. The boy stands before his father, with his hands upon the sword and an awe-struck look upon his face, his position indicating that he had run out to meet his father and was returning with him towards the house.

THE DEAD MOUSE.

As many chairs and tables as can be put upon the stage without crowding should be placed there, in the utmost confusion, some of the chairs lying on the floor, while a dish pan and two or three flat-irons are strewn about. On the different chairs and tables stand half a dozen ladies of various sizes and ages and styles of dress, each holding her skirts tightly around her and apparently out of breath from exertion, armed with some article of female warfare—a broom, a rolling pin, a flat-iron or a poker. In the midst of them stands a very small boy (the smaller the better), holding up a dead mouse by the tail, with a small stick in his other hand.

THE DRUNKARD'S HOME.

In the farthest corner of the stage lies what purports to be a dead woman on some straw. Two weeping children kneel beside the couch. In the foreground are the drunkard and his daughter. She has just snatched a half filled bottle from him and is pointing to the corner.

where the children are kneeling, while he, in a toppling position, look with an idiotic stare in the direction she points. Poverty and distress should be depicted on their faces and in their dress, while the furniture, consisting of two chairs and a table, on which stands an earthenware vessel, should be very dilapidated.

THE FINE ARTS.

SCULPTURE, MUSIC AND PAINTING.

These should be represented by three ladies clothed entirely in white, exactly alike. The dresses should be loose, with flowing sleeves, and slit open from the knee down. White hose and white slippers should be worn. They all wear white wreaths upon their heads. Sculpture stands at the right of the group. Upon a white pedestal beside her stands a small statue. She has a mallet and a sculptor's chisel in her hands. Music stands in the middle with a harp in her hands, while Painting is on the left, with a palette and a brush. They should all stand as if in the act of working in their art. Everything should be painted white—even the ladies' faces.

A SAMPLE OF WIFELY UNSELFISHNESS.—An illustration of true wifely unselfishness comes from Newaygo county, Wis., where a woman, after making a nice little sum of money by picking blackberries, instead of buying a new dress, bought her husband a fiddle.

—A book has recently made its appearance in Boston with the title of "Zobar." It makes a clerk look real angry to have a lady rush in and remark: "Young man do you keep 'Zobar?'"

—"Coming out at the little end of the horn" is all right. It is the thought of never coming out at all that worries the young girl who is over the fence of youth into the garden of society.

—It is reported that Wiggins learned to be a prophet by guessing what his wife would say when he came home late at night.—*Philadelphia Herald.*

The corset is a paradox. It comes to stay, and at the same time goes to waist.

⇒✿EIGHT✿⇐

EXCELLENT REASONS WHY EVERY LADY

SHOULD WEAR

BALL'S CORSETS.

First—They need no breaking in.

Second—Invalids can wear them with ease and comfort, as they yield to every movement of the body.

Third—They do not compress the most vital part of the wearer.

Fourth—They will fit a greater variety of forms than any other make.

Fifth—Owing to their peculiar construction they will last twice as long as an ordinary corset.

Sixth—They have had the unqualified endorsement of every physician who has examined them.

Seventh—They have given universal satisfaction to all ladies who have worn them, the common remark being

"We will Never Wear any Other Make."

Eighth—They are the only Corset that a manufacturer has ever dared to guarantee perfectly satisfactory in every respect to the wearer, or the money refunded.

The wonderful popularity of BALL'S CORSETS has induced rival manufacturers to imitate them and infringe on our patents. If you want a Corset that will give perfect satisfaction, insist on one marked "Patented Feb 22, 1881,"

☞ And See that the Name "BALL" is on the Box.

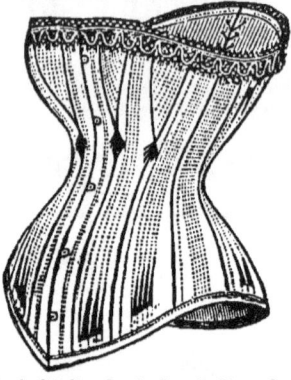 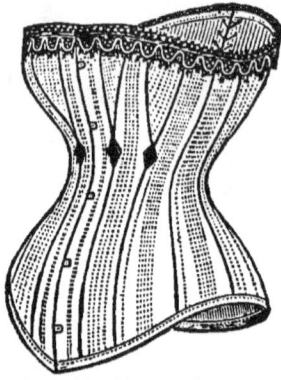

FANCY WORK.

TO MAKE A HANDSOME WORK-CASE.

Any firm material may be used for this purpose. The suggestions we give with regard to color will perhaps be found as good as any. Get a piece of gray or yellow Java canvas, twelve inches long and seven wide with bright colored silk or satin for lining. Feather-stitch the canvas down both sides and across one end, leaving space to turn in the edges. Baste on the lining and finish the edges neatly by turning in and blind-stitching ; or bind them with ribbon to match the silk lining. The feather-stitched end is then pointed by turning down the corners and sewing them together. Turn the lower end up about four inches to form a bag and sew sides together firmly. Make a loop at the point and sew a button on the outside ; so that the case may be rolled up and fastened.

TO MAKE HANDSOME DESIGNS FOR NEAT PIN-CUSHIONS, ETC., ON A SEWING MACHINE.

By folding a cloth repeatedly, and sewing on a machine almost at random, you can often make a very pretty design when the cloth is opened up. As an experiment try the following:

Take a piece of thin, tough paper, about a foot square, and fold the two opposite corners together, forming a triangle; then fold again with the two long corners together. Be sure that the folded edges are even each time you double it. Then fold again so that the four corners are together, making a neat, little right-angled triangle. Now fold once more so that the center of the page is about three-fourths of an inch from the corner. Now remove the thread and shuttle from the machine and sew, or rather punch as crooked a line as you can sew, allowing the stitches to come to the edges of the top fold, but not to run over it. Turn the paper about and stitch back in another direction. Then commence at the center point and run around promiscuously, forming each line into an irregular curve. Open up your paper and you will have a design that will surprise you and pay you for your trouble. To transfer the pattern upon cloth, use it as a stencil, powdering some common bluing through the holes.

BIRD'S NEST PENWIPER.

Cut out of green cloth a half-dozen leaves—almost any small leaf will answer for a pattern. Fasten on a piece of cloth, the points out, in the form of a circle. Then take some worsted or stained cotton batting and form a nest in which by means of sealing wax or glue you fasten four or five peas painted white. After the penwiper has been used for a little while the eggs will appear speckled, caused by the ink spattered upon them.

A PRETTY PENWIPER.

Take the smallest lead pencil you can procure, one from a ball programme perhaps, and sharpen the point. Then take a piece of black cloth and a piece of bright satin, cut in the form of a circle and scollop the edges. Then prick or cut a small hole in the center. Insert the lead pencil so that the satin is on the outside and crease the cloth into the shape of a closed parasol. Secure at the top by tying a small bow of silk ribbon around it, and allow the bottom to spread a little.

ORIGIN OF CRAZY QUILTS.

" Crazy" patchwork originated in the following manner : A certain titled lady while learning embroidery in an English seminary lost her mind, and it became necessary to confine her in a private mad-house. But she still retained her passion for needle-work, and spent most of her time in uniting pieces of material furnished her from the mad-house scrap-bag. Although unable to perform the difficult stitches of embroidery work, it was noticed that in joining the odds and ends of material given her she invariably used contrasting or assimilating colors of thread or silk, and that nearly every stitch was different from the others. Specimens of her work found their way outside of the asylum, and since then millions of women, apparently sane, have found delight in imitating the handiwork of the crazy countess,

ARTIFICIAL ILLUMINATIONS.

A very pleasing exhibition may be made, with very little trouble or expense, in the following manner: Provide a box, which you fit up with architectural designs cut on pasteboard ; prick small holes in those parts of the building where you wish the illuminations to appear, observing, that in proportion to the perspective, the holes are to be made smaller, and on the near objects the holes are to be made larger. Behind these designs thus perforated you fix a lamp or candle, but in such a manner that the reflection of the light shall only shine through the hole; then placing a light of just sufficient brilliance to show the design of the buildings before it, and making a hole for the sight at the front end of the box, you will have a tolerable representation of illuminated buildings.

The best way of throwing the light in front, is to place an oiled paper before it, which will cast a mellow gleam over the scenery, and not dimish the effect of the illumination. This can be very easily planned, both not to obstruct the sight, nor be seen to disadvantage. The lights behind the picture should be very strong ; and if a magnifying glass were placed in the sight hole, it would tend grately to increase the effect. The box must be covered in, leaving an aperture for the smoke of the lights to pass through.

The above exhibition can only be shown at candle-lights; but there is another way, by fixing small pieces of gold on the building instead of drilling the holes, which gives something like the appearance of illumination, but is by no means equal to the foregoing experiment.

N. B.—It would be an improvement if paper of various colors, rendered transparent by oil, were placed between the lights behind the aperture in the buildings, as they would then resemble lamps of different colors.

SHAVING PAPER CASE.

Take a grape leaf, lay it down on card-board, and, drawing around the edges, cut out the pattern. Get some tissue paper of various colors, fold six or eight times, and lay your pattern upon them, and cut to the same shape as your pattern with a sharp knife or pair of shears. These are for wiping the razor. Make the cover of the same form, in green silk, or cloth, or Japanese canvas. Overcast the edge, or bind it with ribbon, and imitate the veins of the leaf with long stitches of green sewing silk. The tissue-paper grape leaves are inserted between the outside leaf covers. There must be a loop of ribbon at the stem end of the leaf to hang it up by.

SOFA-CUSHION COVER.

Get half a yard of white silk canvas, a yard and a half of thick satin ribbon, three inches wide, blue or rose-colored, a few skeins of floss silk, and a silk cord and tassels. Cut the ribbon into three pieces, to be basted at equal distances on the canvas, one in the middle, the others at either side, half-way between the middle and the edge. Feather stitch the ribbon down on both sides with pale yellow floss. In the spaces left between the ribbon stripes, embroider a graceful little pattern in flosses which harmonize with the shade of the ribbon. Make up the cushion with a lining of plain silk or satin, and trim the edge with the cord and tassels. The colors may be different than those given. Black satin ribbon and brilliant embroidery make an effective combination.

A PRETTY EASEL FOR PHOTOGRAPHS.

The following materials are required: A few narrow strips of card-board; some gold paper; a square inch of red merino, flannel or silk; a square inch of blue silk; some tiny bits of blue, yellow, red, green, white, and black paper or woolen goods; and three little sticks of wood. A match will supply two pieces, if whittled down a little thinner; the other must be half an inch long and a quarter of an inch broad. Cut three strips of card-board half an inch wide; two must be nine inches and the other 8⅛ inches long. Bevel the two at the top so that they will fit together like the letter A. Cover all the strips with gold paper, leaving a surplus of paper at the top. When dry punch three or four holes at equal distances in the two strips forming the front of the easel. With thickly melted gum-arabic join the two front pieces; the gold paper must be folded over the top of each strip. Next gum a small piece of wood half an inch long at the back, where these two strips join; then gum the back piece on. The gold paper, which has been left longer than the strips, will now be found useful in fastening all three strips together by gumming the paper. A little red skull-cap, made of merino or silk, covers all sign of patching, and helps to strengthen the whole. The easel-pegs are made by covering the match-like stick of wood first with white and then with gold paper, and are fastened in the easel holes with gum. The palette is cut out of card-board, covered with gilt paper, and has the bits of colored goods pasted on it. It is hung on the peg and fastened with gum. The mahl-stick may be made of a tooth-pick. The gold paper is cut in a narrow strip and wound around the mahl-stick, the end of which is ornamented with a knob, made by cutting a round piece of blue silk, tying it with black silk. Gum the mahl-stick fast to the back of the palette, one end resting on the floor. The piece that lies across the easel, sup-ported by the pegs, is made of card-board, covers with gilt paper and need not be fastened. The palette will keep it in place. Use flour paste for fastening the gilt paper on the card-board. For all the other fastening use gum-arabic.

WASH-STAND FRILLS.

Cut a yard and a quarter of plain or figured white muslin into two breadths, sew them together, and make a hem two inches wide on both edges. Run a thread all across one end, half an inch below the hem; into this put some tape, and draw up the frill, leaving a knot in the tape at each end. The ruffle is to be nailed to the wall through these knots, above the wash-stand, where the wall paper is in danger of being spat-tered when persons are washing. Make two pretty bows of the ribbon and pin them over the tape ends. You can draw up the lower part of the muslin piece also if you wish, so as to make the top and bottom just alike.

TABLE AND CHAIR COVERS OF STAMPED LINEN.

These covers are made of coarse gray linen like that used for kitchen table cloths. One of the best patterns to choose is that very common one which is lined off into diamonds, with a star in the middle of each diamond. Divide these stars into groups of four, six, or eight, and work each star with Berlin worsted of a different color, tak-ing care that your colors harmonize with each other and make a good general effect. When all the stars are embroidered sew narrow black velvet ribbon over the lines which form the diamonds. If for a table cover, trim the edges with a row of black velvet ribbon, a fringe or a cord with tassels in the corners.

THE FIRST CORSET.

Planche's Cyclopædia of Costume says the word "corse," "corses," or "corset" was first met with in the fourteenth century, and was applied to a close-fitting garment or a pair of stays, though in that time it evidently indicated an outer vestment. In the wardrobe account of Edward III, there is an entry of "a corse of red velvet with eagles and garters for the queen," and mention of "corsets of cloth furred," given by the king to Queen Phillippa.

M. Viollet-le-Duc has a long article on this subject, in which he quotes numerous passages from the French chronicles, wardrobe accounts and other documents, showing that a garment called a "corset" was worn in France from the time of St. Louis to the commencement of the fifteenth century, by both sexes and all classes; that it varied in length, shape and amplitude; that it was lined occasionally with fur, and had sleeves of every imaginable description.

The jupon of the fourteenth century was the military garment which succeeded to the surcoat of the thirteenth. It fitted the body tightly, and was worn over a steel breast-plate, which, at that period, was also called a corset. The term was generally applied to various garments worn by men as well as by women, and all possessing the peculiar feature of closely fitting the person from the neck to the waist. The name corset was applied during the fourteenth and fifteenth centuries to various similar articles of dress, also known as the "kirtle," the "cote-hardie," the "jacket," the "doublet," and the "pourpoint." By the sumptuary laws of Edward IV, the wives of esquires and gentlemen, knight-bachelors, and knights under the rank of lord, unless they were knights of the Garter, were forbidden to wear cloth of gold, velvet upon velvet, furs of sable, or "any kind of corses" worked with gold; and women of inferior rank were prohibited from wearing "any corse of silk" made out of the realm.

Something like a bodice appears about this time, the body of the dress being laced in front over a stomacher, as in Switzerland and other parts of the eastern continent it is seen to this day.

Ever since the time of Edward III. penurious costumers have been busy in modeling changes in the style and construction of this almost indispensable article of female apparel, until the world is deluged with contrivances of every imaginable description, most of them, however, better adapted for the purpose of coining money for the inventor and to make business for the doctors and undertakers, than to give health, comfort and beauty to the wearer. It remained for Dr. Ball to give to the world his now famous Health Preserving Corset, which possesses all the merits of all the known styles since Queen Phillippa donned her kirtle, up to the time when the more modern costumers attempted to steal his patents and rob him of his well-earned success ; but it embraces besides a principle which, instead of being destructive of female loveliness by painting the face with the hue of death, adds grace to the body, contour and dignity to the figure, and the glow and beauty of health to the cheek of the wearer. A corset with coiled wire spring sections that a woman cannot use as an instrument of torture, while she gets all the benefit of substantial support and stay, is a godsend; and such a corset has only been produced in the nineteenth century.— *Tribune.*

PAINFUL STATE OF UNCERTAINTY.

We have heard a number of good things on "dudes," but none better than on one who, for some incomprehensible reason, was married one day last week to a stout, healthy country girl. The dude was perfumed, wore frills on his shirt, had his hair curled, and he presented such a feminine appearance that the clergyman said:

"I don't want to make any mistake about this business, so which of you is the bride, anyhow?"—*Potter County (Pa.) Journal.*

We feel that our Corsets need only be known to the ladies to insure their gratitude and our success. Our confidence in this fact is such that we offer the following guarantee on *all* the goods we make:

We hereby *guarantee* every one of Ball's Coiled Spring Elastic Section Corsets as *perfectly satisfactory* in every respect to the wearer, or the money paid for it will be refunded by the person from whom it was bought, if it has not been worn to exceed three weeks.

These Corsets are for sale by first-class dry goods dealers everywhere, but if not found in your town will be forwarded by mail, as shown inside.

In ordering please state style, size, and color wanted.

DEATH FROM TIGHT LACING.

Glasgow News.

The evils of tight lacing were shown at an inquest which was held last week at Kilburn, upon the body of Mrs. Amelia Jury. Dr. Hill stated that upon making a post-mortem examination he found that the stomach was contracted in the middle by a firm band, narrowing it to one-eighth of the usual size, so there were virtually two stomachs, and this contraction was on a level with a deep indentation on the liver, corresponding to where the stays were tightly bound round. The liver itself was flattened out, and was driven down very deep into the pelvis also, and there was no doubt but what this was also produced by tight lacing. The Coroner said that he some time ago held an inquest where it was shown that the liver had been very seriously injured through tight lacing, and perhaps these cases would act as a caution against the practices now adopted.

A LESSON IN PRONUNCIATION.

" How do you pronounce d-o, Mr. Featherly?" inquired Bobby, at the dinner table.

" Do, Bobby," replied Mr. Featherly, indulgently.

"How do you pronounce d-e-w?" continued Bobby.

"D-u-e-w," and here Mr. Featherly put on a genteel air for the benefit of Bobby's big sister.

" Well, then, how would you pronounce the second day of the week?"

" Tewsday, I think."

" You're wrong."

" Wrong? How would you pronounce the second day of the week?"

" Monday."

—A little girl, visiting a neighbor with her mother, was gazing curiously at the hostess' new bonnet, when the owner queried: " Do you like it, Laura?" The innocent replied: " Why, mother said it was a perfect fright, but it don't scare me!"

—Lightning-rod agent—"It's dangerous to be under this tree in a thunder-storm. One of us might get killed." Victim—"Well, if you are killed you won't be able to talk any more, and if I am killed I can't hear you. So I guess we'd better stay."

WHAT EMINENT PHYSICIANS SAY OF BALL'S CORSETS.

MOREHOUSE PARISH, La., Aug. 15, 1884.

CHICAGO CORSET CO.:

My wife is especially pleased with Ball's Corset. She says it fits like an old glove, and it is perfectly easy. Allow me to congratulate you on making the best corset I ever saw.

DR. BEN. H. BRODNAX.

———

OSKALOOSA, IOWA, Aug. 21, 1883.

CHICAGO CORSET CO.:

Score another compliment for your Corset. One of our prominent lady singers says she will not allow any of her quartette to sing in any other kind but BALL'S HEALTH-PRESERVING CORSET.

WILLARD & WEEKS CO.

———

ATCHISON, KAN., Oct. 15, 1884.

CHICAGO CORSET CF.:

The Corset that you sent my wife pleases her better than any she has ever had, and I consider Ball's Corsets the most perfectly arranged for health of anything of the kind I have ever examined. You can hereafter consider her a customer of yours for corsets.

DR. A. N. SPRAGUE.

———

MARYSVILLE, OHIO, Aug. 16, 1884.

CHICAGO CORSET CO.:

I want one of your Circle Hip Corsets. I am a practicing physician, and will cheerfully recommend the Corset to my patrons. I am sorry I have to wait over Sunday, I am so anxious to get the very best Corset that ever was made. I feel anxious about the man who composed all that poetry. Is he living, and in comfortable health? Now, I am passionately fond of music, and if I can only find a composer capable of writing a grand symphony to which I can sing those words, and at the same time keep those beautiful pictures before me, I shall die content—especially if the Corset suits, which of course it will.

Very respectfully,   MRS. ANNA HOYT, M.D.

LADIES!

If you appreciate a Corset that will neither break down nor roll up IN WEAR,

TRY BALL'S CORSETS.

If you value health and comfort,

WEAR BALL'S CORSETS.

If you desire a Corset that fits the first day you wear it, and needs no "breaking in,"

BUY BALL'S CORSETS.

If you desire a Corset that yields with every motion of the body,

EXAMINE BALL'S CORSETS.

If you want a perfect fit and support without compression,

USE BALL'S CORSETS.

Owing to their peculiar construction it is imbossible to break steels in Ball's Csrsets.

The Elastic Sectiona in Ball's Corsets contain no rubber, and are warrented to outwear the Corset.

Every Pair Sold with the Following Guarantee:

"If not perfectly satisfactory in every respect after three weeks' trial, the money paid for them will be refunded (by the dealer), SOILED OR UNSOILED."

Look out for worthless imitations. See that the name "BALL" is on the box, also guarantee of Chicago Corset Company.

CAUTION.

The wonderful popularity of **BALL'S CORSETS** has induced rival manufacturers to imitate them and infringe on our patents. If you want a Corset that will give perfect satisfaction, insist on one marked "Patented February 22, 1881," and boned with **K A B O**, which is the only **CORSET** Stiffener treated by **FLORSHEIM'S SECRET PROCESS**, and therefore unbreakable, and

See that the Name "**BALL**" is on the Box.

Testimony of MRS. J. PARRY, of the Mapleson Opera Company.

Palmer House
Chicago. —
April 8/85

Chicago Corset Co.
I fully recommend Ballo
Corset as being best-adapted
to singers or in fact anyone
wishing to have a comfortable
Corset —

Mrs J. Parry
Mapleson Opera Co

PALMISTRY.

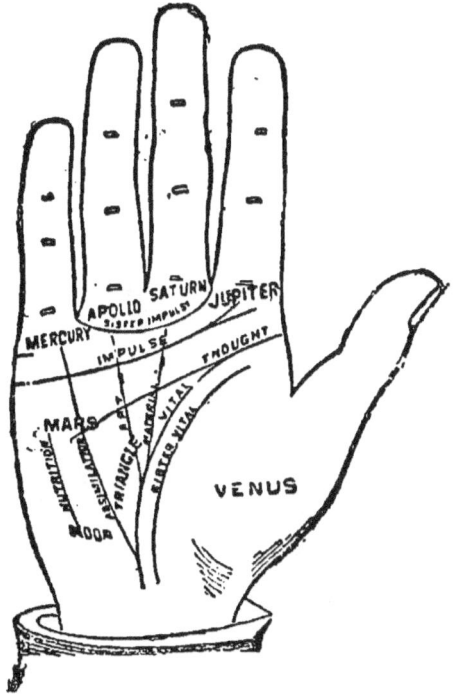

MAP OF THE HAND.

In reading fortunes by the hand not only must the lines on the palm be observed and studied, but the general shape, appearance and texture of the entire hand and of the different parts should be noted, as well as the prominences on the palm designated above by the names of the planets.

The entire hand should first be observed.

Small hands show the man who plans; large hands the man who performs. Long hands an appreciation and performance of detail;

short hands a broad grasp of generalities. Hard hands show strong muscular power and enduring activity. Elastic or sinewy hands show energy rather than endurance, vitality without proportionate muscular power, a tendency to mass the entire strength into brief and effective effort. The soft hand shows little muscular power, but grace and activity in light labor. The plastic, or soft, non-elastic hand, shows a lack of endurance, a low state of vitality and muscular power, weakness, pass-

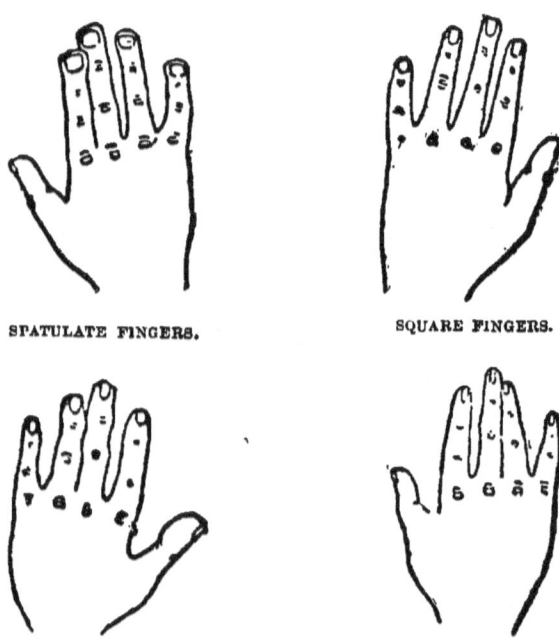

SPATULATE FINGERS.

SQUARE FINGERS.

KNOTTED FINGERS.

TAPERING FINGERS.

ivity, and possibly disease. Hard hands show an appreciation for practical realities; soft hands an appreciation of the imaginative faculties. If the palm is thin, skinny, and narrow it denotes a feeble mind, a narrow intellect, a general feebleness and flabbiness of character. If the palm is firm and well-proportioned it indicates intelligence, will power and an evenly-balanced mind. Again, if it is so wide and strong as to be out of proportion with the fingers, the thumb, and the rest of the body, it indicates selfishness and sensuality; while going still farther in the same direction it indicates brutality unrestrained by intelligence. A hollow hand denotes failure and misfortune. It is always the rule that the normal and well-proportioned hand is the best.

The fingers are then examined.

"Knotted" fingers—that is, fingers in which the joints are so developed as to show a perceptible bulge—indicate logical thought or deduction and a desire for order and proof. Smooth fingers signify perception, intention, and rapid determination. Tapering fingers show the rule of the ideal—the more tapering the more idealistic. Painters, sculptors, musicians or poets will have smooth, tapering fingers, with full, oval finger-tips. Pointed finger-tips show the same qualities erratically used. Square-tipped fingers attest a mind and hand working in unison, the brain directing the hand and the hand obeying the brain in constant work for definite ends. Square-ended and slightly knotted fingers are characteristics of most celebrated men. Spatulate or stubbed fingers indicate a desire for manual labor or muscular effort. Large, ungainly fingers, of the same size at the end as at the roots, index one who is an unthinking plodder and drudge, short fingers see the mass and judge of the whole, long fingers see the individual parts and by them form an estimate.

The nails must also be studied. Long nails indicate a peacemaker or one who is steadfast in friendship, or one who wants to see only the good, or one who is skilled in diplomacy. Short nails indicate self-assertion; with the skin high upon them they suggest pugnacity, mockery, or frivolity; with a large thumb they indicate malice and irritation. Broad nails indicate gentleness and submission. Narrow nails show activity and a love of excitement, and suggest a mischievous and tyrannical disposition. Round nails show an honest disposition and a quick temper; if very small and round they show obstinate anger and hatred. Fan-shaped nails announce envy and vanity.

Then study the palm carefully. Notice first the three chief lines of the hand. The vital line, or line of life, encircles the ball of the thumb, or Mount of Venus. The thought line, or line of head, starts from the line of life (to which it is usually joined) between the thumb and first finger, and runs in an approximately straight line across the hand. The impulse line, or line of heart, starts from the Mount of Jupiter or Saturn and runs across the hand as the boundary line of the Mounts of Saturn, Apollo, and Mercury. These three lines represent respectively, vitality, intellect, and affection. Chief of the secondary lines is the material line, or line of fortune, also called the line of fate, which starts down near the wrist, either from the line of life (as in the map) or further towards the Mount of the Moon, and runs towards the Mount of Saturn, near or upon which it generally ends. The line of art and brilliancy rises at or near the line of life and runs to or over the Mount of Apollo. The assimilation line, or line of health, rises near the wrist and runs across the line of thought in the direction of the Mount of Mercury. The line of nutrition, also called the Milky Way, traverses the Mount of the Moon parallel to the assimilation line. The sister vital line, or line of Mars, lies inside the line of life. The sister impulse line, or Girdle of Venus, begins mostly between the little and third fingers and incloses or traverses the Mounts of Apollo and Saturn, ending between the middle and index fingers.

See if the mounts are in proper proportion, and, if not, then towards what other mounts they are deflected. Next as to the condition of the mounts, whether large, moderate, or depressed. Next their relation to the lines—the principal, secondary, or minor lines—which point towards, touch or traverse them. Mounts are favorable when they are generous, smooth, well-rounded, and connected with the appropriate lines. The Mount of Venus, in connection with the vital line, shows the physical man, his strength, intensity, endurance and force. Venus favorable indicates a prime physical manhood, but whether this manhood is used to a good purpose must be determined by the tendencies and abilities shown in the other parts of the hand. All lines on the mount that are parallel with the vital lines indicate a legitimate and healthy use of the strength, while lines at right angle indicate irritation and excess. Jupiter favorable indicates ideality, sensitiveness, refinement, and enthusiasm. It may, therefore, according as the other parts of the hand determine, indicate religious fervor, worthy ambition, honor, self-respect, ardent affections, a love of the beautiful in nature or art, or other desires founded upon impressionability. Jupiter weak and depressed indicates a mind devoid of imagination or versatility. The Mount of Saturn indicates realism, seriousness, and intensity of purpose. Favorable it shows industry, prudence and energy, and success through these qualities if success be possible. This mount depressed or absent shows an easy-going, careless disposition.

The Mount of Apollo, when favorable, indicates taste and ability in the arts. Mercury favorable indicates a love of clear, exact, full knowledge. It shows promptness, clearness, logical persuasiveness. When excessively high it denotes pretentious arrogance. Absent or depressed it shows awkwardness and diffidence. The Mount of Mars, when favorable, indicates courage, coolness and fearlessness in danger. Mars excessive will suggest foolhardiness and cruelty. The Mount of the Moon denotes vague, restless desires, and an inclination for melancholy and solitude.

Lines must be read according to their position, length, continuity, development, color, and shape. By development is meant their direction after being joined or intersected by another line. The vital line (the instructions for which will serve as a key for the interpretation of all the other lines) represents the life of the individual. This line in connection with the formation of the Mount of Venus gives the key to the physical condition of the subject, and as the intellect and affections, as well as the fortune, are to some degree dependent on the physical condition for their proper development the meaning of the value of this line must be borne in mind when interpreting the other lines and mounts. The vital line clearly drawn and well-formed, without breaks or cuts, and continuing completely round the Mount of Venus until it unites with the wrist-line, denotes vigorous health, a good constitution, freedom from dangerous diseases, and consequently long life. If the line is double, or has a sister line, it shows an exceptionally vigorous existence. If the line is long and slender it indicates low vitality and doubtful health. If this slender line is red it shows irritability of temperament; if pale, it shows sluggishness of the blood and a lack of endurance. A healthy flesh-color is the normal condition. If the line is broad and pale it indicates a tendency to diseases of the digestive organs; if broad and livid it shows a tendency to heart disease. If the line is splintered or chained it indicates painful diseases. If broken by many little lines it shows numerous sicknesses or troubles that have become chronic. Severe sicknesses leave their record on this line. The age at which sickness or accident occurred or at the age at which sickness or accident is threatened may be approximately determined by the location of the cut, break or change on the vital line—the line not only recording the dangers safely passed but those that lurk in the future.

Branches toward the Mount of Jupiter indicate ambition and success. Branches must be interpreted by the character of the mounts toward which they tend. The connection of the life and thought lines show life and thought in harmony and vice versa. The life line bifurcated near the wrist suggests brain troubles. A clear and direct thought-line signifies a lucid mind in a healthy brain. Curving towards the Mount of the Moon it indicates a capricious fancy. The strength and intensity of the affections are proportionate to the strength and clearness of the line of impulse or heart. If the line runs clear across the hand it indicates an excess of affection which runs to jealousy. A chained line indicates flirtations. Breaks denote inconstancy. Intersections by little cross lines indicate unfortunate love affairs. The line of fortune, when it starts from the line of life, indicates that the luck in life is the result of personal merit. Starting from the Mount of the Moon it shows that the fortune is due to the affection or caprice of the opposite sex. If straight and of good color from the line of heart toward the fingers it denotes good fortune in the later years of life. The line of fortune is divided into periods, as in the line of life. From the wrist to the line of thought represents the first thirty years of life; from the line of thought to the line of impulse shows the fortune between the ages of 30 and 45; and from the line of impulse to the end of the line toward the fingers shows the fortune to the end of life.

A BIG CORSET FACTORY.

A noted industry of Aurora, Ill., a city of extensive industries, is the Chicago Corset Company's factory, employing 800 operatives in the manufacture of Ball's famous Health Preserving Corset. In the erection and fitting up of the factory, which is of brick, 200x150 feet in size and four stories in height, $75,000 was expended. On the east side of the building are the engine and boiler rooms—an addition 22x34 feet. The ground upon which it is located is owned by the company, and is 297x170 feet in size, upon which it is designed in the future to erect the large buildings of an immense factory, of which the present structure will be but one wing. The building is well lighted, containing about 250 double windows. Careful attention is given every sanitary consideration throughout the entire building. Each story is 12 feet from floor to ceiling, the ascent being made by broad stairways. All goods are handled by a steam elevator. All woodwork is covered with fire-proof paint, and the upper story contains a large cistern of water, from which connections are made with each floor. The gas used about the premises is manufactured on the grounds from gasoline,

The first floor contains the office, cloak-room, stock-room, and shipping-room. The second and third floors will be devoted exclusively to sewing machines, each floor being intended to accommodate between three and four hundred operatives, the majority of whom are women. On the third floor are 300 of the " I. F." Singer sewing machines, and 150 on the second floor. The fourth floor contains some of the intricate machinery for coiling wire and preparing other portions of Ball's famous Health Preserving Corset, and also the cutting table. This table is an elaborate and costly piece of furniture, one hundred feet in length by three in width, constructed of small blocks of wood five inches in length securely glued together, so that the cutting surface is composed of the ends of these blocks. Forty-eight thicknesses of the fabric being spread upon this table, the brass patterns are tacked upon it and the cutting is speedily and skillfully executed with a knife. Aside from the Singer machines, nearly every piece of machinery used in the manufacture of this corset is the invention of Mr. T. H. Ball, the senior partner and manager of the establishment, and some portions of it are very interesting.

Power is furnished by a fifty horse-power engine. The company have for some time had a large factory in operation in Chicago, but the increasing demand for its product rendered necessary an enlargement of manufacturing facilities. Hence the establishment of the Aurora factory.

The demand for Ball's Corsets was so great, that the Company has been obliged to open another factory at Joliet, Ill., where they employ 200 operatives, and have 100 Singer sewing machines running.—*Chicago Times.*

TIGHT LACING.

Mr. Richard A. Proctor, the well-known lecturer on astronomy, once tried the experiment of wearing a corset, and thus describes the result : "When the subject of corset wearing was under discussion in the pages of the *English Mechanic*, I was struck," he says, "with the apparent weight of evidence in favor of tight-lacing. I was in particular struck by the evidence of some as to its use in reducing corpulence. I was corpulent. I also was disposed, as I am still, to take an interest in scientific experiment. I thought I would give this matter a fair trial. I read all the instructions, carefully followed them, and varied the time of applying pressure with that 'perfectly stiff busk' about which correspondents were so enthusiastic. I was foolish enough to try the thing for a matter of four weeks. Then I laughed at myself as a hopeless idiot, and determined to give up the attempt to reduce by artificial means that superabundance of fat on which only starvation and much exercise, or the air of America, has ever had any real reducing influences. But I was reckoning without my host. ·As the Chinese lady suffers, I am told, when her feet-bindings are taken off, and as the flat-head baby howls when his head-boards are removed, so for a while was it with me. I found myself manifestly better in stays. I laughed at myself no longer. I was too angry with myself to laugh. I would as soon have condemned myself to using crutches all the time, as to wearing always a busk. But for my one month of folly I had to endure three months of discomfort. At the end of about that time I was my own man again.

COME AGAIN.

"There's a man with a club in the office down stairs, looking for the editor," remarked the office-boy, coolly, to the boss of the sanctum, as he walked in and set the towel up in the corner.

"Good Lord !" groaned the editor. "Are you sure?"

"Yes," replied the boy. "He was looking for the editor; that's what he said."

"What kind of a man was he?"

"Tough, country-jake sort of a chap, as big as a skinned hoss, and hands on him like hams," answered the boy, with a wicked smile.

"What kind of a club did he have ; was it anything like a dray-pin?" suggested the editor, watching the door, nervously.

"Wait till I go and see," said the boy, kindly.

In a few minutes he returned.

"Well?" queried the editor, mopping the cold perspiration up with a last year's blotter, "Well?"

!"Ugh !" grunted the boy, in a disappointed tone ; "it was a club of twenty new subscribers."

Then the editor kicked the boy gleefully, and ordered him to bring the man up.

Said a little Brooklyn boy who was watering the flowers in his mother's garden with his latest acquisition, a watering pot: "Now, God, you take care of the rest of the ground, and I'll attend to this little patch!"